"What di̶d̶ ̶$̶5̶.̶0̶0̶
Wesley aske Secret Life of Dr. Demented

At the sink, Mr. Wh̶
he saw what Wesley v̶
open.

Wesley saw the expression on Mr. Wheeler's face. He looked at the black leather mask in his hand. He thought about Mr. Wheeler limping. He thought about the night before. He looked at the muscles on Mr. Wheeler's arms. And he came to a conclusion, the only conclusion that made any sense at all.

"You're Dr. Demented!"

Wesley couldn't believe what he had just discovered. Mr. Wheeler, the friendly guy down the street who taught gym at Nimitz High, led a secret life as Dr. Demented, the meanest, cruelest, and most violent man in the AWF.

THE SECRET LIFE OF DR. DEMENTED

Dan Gutman

AN ARCHWAY PAPERBACK
Published by POCKET BOOKS
New York   London   Toronto   Sydney   Singapore

For information regarding special discounts for bulk purchases, please contact Simon & Schuster Special Sales at 1-800-456-6798 or business@simonandschuster.com

This book is a work of fiction. Names, characters, places and incidents are products of the author's imagination or are used fictitiously. Any resemblance to actual events or locales or persons, living or dead, is entirely coincidental.

AN ARCHWAY PAPERBACK *Original*

An Archway Paperback published by
POCKET BOOKS, a division of Simon & Schuster, Inc.
1230 Avenue of the Americas, New York, NY 10020

ISBN: 0-7434-2704-1

First Archway Paperback printing September 2001

10 9 8 7 6 5 4 3 2 1

AN ARCHWAY PARPERBACK and colophon are registered trademarks of Simon & Schuster, Inc.

Cover art by Doron Ben-Ami

Printed in the U.S.A.

IL 4+

Acknowledgment

Thanks to Bill Apter, Scott Keith, Michael Malinsky, Stephen Valentini, and Cathy Williamson for their help in gathering the information for this book.

THE
SECRET LIFE
OF
DR.
DEMENTED

1

Heels and Babyfaces

"I'M GONNA RIP YOUR HEAD OFF, DOCTOR Demented!" Sergeant America shouted hoarsely into the microphone. "And I'm gonna take that ugly mask off with it! Then we'll see who you really are!"

Sergeant America stood motionless in the center of the ring, with one well-muscled arm pointing toward the door of the "ready room," where the wrestlers got dressed. A single spotlight illuminated him. The rest of the Houston Astrodome was in darkness.

"Die Doctor Demented!" chanted fifteen thousand rabid professional wrestling fans at once, shaking the building. *"Die Doctor Demented!"*

The despised Dr. Demented had yet to emerge from the ready room, where he was sipping from a bottle of carrot juice while thumbing through the latest issue of *Better Homes and Gardens* magazine.

"A week ago during SkullCrush in Dallas," Sergeant America continued over the crowd noise, "my lovely wife Erica left me and ran off with you."

"Booooooooooooooo!" screamed the fifteen thousand. The fans hated Dr. Demented, but they loved having Dr. Demented to hate.

Hoping to get on TV, many fans were holding up banners and cardboard signs they had made: DEATH TO DR. DEMENTED. WE HATE DR. DEMENTED! GIVE BACK MRS. AMERICA. And so on.

"Well, Doctor Demented, I'm here tonight to win Erica back!"

"Yeaaaaaaaaaaaaaah!"

Erica America's real name was Wendy Blau. She was a struggling actress who took the Erica America role because it paid better than waitressing.

Sergeant America, whose real name was Bill Anderson, let the booing die down before continuing. He had only been Sergeant America for a few months, but he was enjoying it immensely. Before he became Sergeant America, he had wrestled under the name Roadkill. Before that, he was Urban Legend. And before that, he had been part of a tag team called Hurricane and Tornado: The Natural Disasters.

None of those characters had caught on big with wrestling fans, so the AWF (American Wrestling Federation) had informed Anderson that his career as a professional wrestler would be over unless he could create a character the fans would respond to more.

Bill Anderson had always loved being a "heel." That is, a bad guy. But the AWF (usually dubbed "awful") suggested he might be more popular as a "babyface"—a good guy. Because of Anderson's all-American looks, the AWF decided he would become Sergeant America and fight for truth, justice, and the American way.

In the early days of pro wrestling, there were lots of babyface wrestlers. But lately, just about all wrestlers were heels to one degree or another. There hadn't been a real "I love America" character in a long time, and the AWF decided it was time to revive the classic good versus evil story line.

Anderson liked changing characters every year or so. It kept the job new and exciting. Even though babyfaces earned less money than heels, he had to admit it was nice to hear the crowd boo the *other* guy for a change.

Sergeant America stood in the middle of the ring wearing nothing but red, white, and blue trunks and a large top hat that had been painted to resemble an American flag. His chest had been carefully shaved and oiled to shine when the spotlight reflected off it.

Anderson was proud of his bulging muscles, having been a bodybuilder for years and taken enormous amounts of muscle-building supplements to make himself resemble a Greek god. He had discovered there was little money in bodybuilding, so he turned to professional wrestling five years ago. As a wrestler, he had millions of fans, his own web site, and he was earning two hundred thousand dollars a year plus a nice cut of the T-shirt sales.

"It's one thing to steal my wife, Doctor Demented," Sergeant America continued, "but worse than that, you insulted the United States of America!"

"*Boooooooooooooooooooooooooooo!*"

In the ready room, Dr. Demented yawned, flipping through *Better Homes and Gardens* until his eye was caught by an article on how to make the perfect walnut-pear sour cream cake.

Dr. Demented also loved being a heel, and he loved being Dr. Demented. It was the only character he had played since starting in pro wrestling. He could hear Sergeant America's rantings through a small speaker above the ready room door.

"The Star Spangled Banner" started blaring over the sound system inside the Astrodome.

"Doctor Demented, you ripped our American flag to pieces in Dallas last week. You threw apple pies at the crowd. You said that you despise children, small animals, and democracy. You reject everything that good Americans stand for—the American way of life."

4

"Boooooooooooooooooooooooooooooo!"

"Well, let me tell you something, Doctor Demented. We didn't let the British kick us around in the Revolutionary War. We didn't let the Germans kick us around in World War II. We didn't let the Russians kick us around in the Cold War. And we're not going to let you kick us around now."

"Yeeeeeeeaaaaaaaaaaaaah!"

"As a citizen and representative of this great nation, I will personally kick your butt all the way to the Gulf of Mexico for the good people of Houston tonight! And in doing so, my wife will see who is the better man!"

"Kick his butt!" screamed fifteen thousand angry Texans. *"Kick his butt!"*

Sergeant America was proud of the references to the British, Germans, and Russians. A history buff, he had come up with the idea in the shower that morning and rehearsed his lines with the AWF writers that afternoon.

"I'm talking to *you*, Doctor Demented!" Sergeant America shouted, his voice rising. "Or are you too *chicken* to come out here and stand up for your twisted beliefs?"

"Chicken! Chicken! Chicken! Chicken!"

In the ready room, Dr. Demented sighed and slipped the magazine into his gym bag. He carefully put on the black mask that covered his head, tying it in the back so it would be secure.

*   *   *

"Do you think Doctor Demented is gonna show?" Jimmy Erdman yelled in Wesley Brown's ear. The boys, both fourteen years old, had seats in the upper level of the Astrodome. They were best friends, and really, each was the other's only friend.

Jimmy was a big, heavyset boy with a crew cut. Wesley, much shorter and very skinny, had red hair and freckles. They traded their pair of binoculars back and forth so they could get a better view of the ring.

"Of course he's gonna show," replied Wesley. "Sergeant America wouldn't be saying all that stuff if Doctor Demented wasn't sitting in the dressing room right now. He's waiting until the timing is right."

"You boys want to go get some cotton candy before the show starts?" asked Jimmy's dad, who had gotten the tickets and driven the boys from their homes in Humble, Texas.

"This *is* the show, Mr. Erdman!" Wesley said, rolling his eyes. Jimmy's dad was not tuned in to the fine points of professional wrestling. Wesley and Jimmy were such devoted fans that they watched three hours of wrestling on TV every Monday night while taping two hours on another channel, so they wouldn't miss a minute of mayhem.

Sergeant America walked around the ring chuckling and making chicken noises into the microphone, taunting Dr. Demented.

"I guess Doctor Demented couldn't make it

tonight!" chortled Sergeant America. "Maybe he got tied up in traffic. Maybe he had a previous engagement. Or just maybe—" Sergeant America put a long dramatic pause here—"just maybe . . . he's afraid!"

"Ooooooooooooooooooooooooooooh!"

The crowd noise had built up to the point where it was impossible to hear what the person one seat away was saying. People were screaming, chanting, booing, stamping their feet and smacking metal objects together.

Music was blasting out of the Astrodome speakers. Nobody could make it out, but it was Wagner's "Ride of the Valkyrie."

When the noise level had reached its crest, a blazing bright white spotlight appeared at the far end of the arena. Into the circle of light stepped . . . Dr. Demented.

2

Ruler of
Our Pathetic World

IT DIDN'T SEEM POSSIBLE THAT IT COULD
get any louder in the Astrodome. But when Dr.
Demented stepped into the spotlight, the place
nearly exploded with noise. Grown men put their
hands over their ears while shouting his name.
Some young children, who were up past their bed-
times and shouldn't have been there in the first
place, began to cry. The noise was too intense for
their delicate ears.

On either side of Dr. Demented, Roman candles
were ignited and shot majestically into the air.
Giant sparklers sent showers of sparks on and
around Dr. Demented. He didn't flinch.

Multicolored lasers swirled pinpoints of light
around the Astrodome. Smoke machines poured
out artificial fog until a layer of it filled the path
leading from Dr. Demented to the ring. Purple
spotlights gave the arena an eerie, otherworldly

glow. Dr. Demented's body filled the video screens that had been placed around the arena.

"It's him!" Wesley Brown marveled. "Doctor Demented!"

Wesley and Jimmy had been serious wrestling fans for several years. They read all the magazines, rented the pay-per-view specials, bought the T-shirts and other memorabilia. But neither boy had been to a professional wrestling match in person. They were in awe.

Dr. Demented stood rock solid in one spot. He let the emotions of the crowd wash over him.

"I hope you choke on some poisoned food and die, Doctor Demented!" a lady screamed into a bullhorn.

"Marry me, Doctor Demented!" hollered another.

Even from their distant seats, Wesley and Jimmy could see the huge muscles that seemed to be trying to push right through the man's skin. Dr. Demented was even bigger than Sergeant America. His shoulder muscles were so built up that it looked like he didn't have a neck.

"He is *cut*, man!" Wesley declared. Jimmy knew what his friend meant, but his dad did not. The boys explained that being "cut" meant that your muscles were sharply defined, as if your body were chiseled from stone.

Dr. Demented's costume was basic black. Black trunks. Black boots. Black mask that completely covered his head except for his eyes, nose, and mouth, like a ski mask. It was made from leather. He looked like a homicidal maniac, which is exactly what the AWF made him out to be.

Dr. Demented held a cordless microphone in his right hand. Slowly, in a voice that sounded like death itself, he spoke the words he used every time he stepped into a wrestling arena. The crowd recited those words with him. . . .

"I . . . RULE . . . THIS . . . PATHETIC . . . WORLD!"

The crowd erupted in another earsplitting burst of boos that sounded like a jet engine revving up.

"Shut yer stinkin' mouths, ya losers!" Dr. Demented shouted at the crowd. "Erica America is *my* woman now, and I'm gonna keep her! Right, baby?"

A gorgeous woman with dark hair and a low-cut red dress ran out and wrapped herself around Dr. Demented. That made the crowd scream even louder. Dr. Demented waited a few seconds until he could be heard.

"I fear no man," he boomed. "I *am* the man. If that *wimp* is the best man America can come up with to represent this country, it's no wonder his wife would rather be with me, a *real* man. I feel sorry for your country. Sergeant America will be spending the night in the hospital. And Erica America will be spending it with *me*. Right, baby?"

"Boooooooooooooooooooooooooooooo!"

"I don't *think* so, Doctor Demented," boomed Sergeant America from the ring. "At the end of the evening, Erica will be with me. And you will come to me and bow before me. No, more than that, you will get on your knees and beg for my permission to allow you to exist. Because if Doctor Demented doesn't beg, Doctor Demented is gonna need a *real* doctor, real bad."

"Ooooooooooooooooooooooooooooh!"

"I get on my knees before nobody," replied Dr. Demented. "You hear me, Sergeant America? When I get through with you, you're gonna wish *you* never existed!"

With that, Dr. Demented handed the microphone to Erica America and sprinted up the aisle. He leaped into the ring and tackled Sergeant America, grabbing him around the waist. Sergeant America powered out of the hold and threw Dr. Demented against the ropes. Demented clotheslined him on the way back, dropping Sergeant America on his back.

The two men went at it furiously for the next few minutes. Chokeslams. Moonsaults. Jackhammers. Combinations. One wrestler would have the advantage momentarily, then his opponent would battle back until he was on top. Several times the referee reached a two count, but each time the man on the bottom would kick his way out of it.

The crowd was roaring, screaming, exploding emotionally with each violent blow.

Any one of these blows, if struck with full force, would knock a man senseless and perhaps kill him. But Dr. Demented and Sergeant America were professionals.

They knew how to hit a man to create a loud smacking noise without putting their full weight behind the blow. They knew how to collide chest to chest; flat part of the body against flat part of the body, so nobody got hurt.

They knew how to jump and miss their target by an inch. They knew how to fly through the air and land without letting the sharp, vulnerable parts of the body—elbows, knees, or head—strike the mat first. Through years of practice, they'd learned how to spread each fall over the largest area of the body possible to prevent injury.

Finally, they knew how to react to each blow and fall to make it look like they'd been hit with a sledgehammer.

Using all this knowledge, neither man suffered a scratch.

"Oh no!" Erica America shrieked into the microphone every time Sergeant America took a hit. "Stop hurting my husband!"

After a few minutes of fast-paced action, Sergeant America gained the upper hand. He had Dr. Demented facedown on the mat, and he was sitting on his back.

"Kids," Sergeant America exhorted as Dr. Demented lay on the mat. "Don't try this at home."

Then he unleashed a "powerbomb." He picked Dr. Demented up by his legs, squeezed Demented's head between his thighs, then dropped him, head-first, to the mat. Dr. Demented lay on his stomach, twitching.

"And don't try this at home either," Sergeant America growled.

Then he did a double arm DDT. He grabbed Dr. Demented's arms behind his back, then sat on his head, driving it into the mat.

"Or this!"

Then he did a standing drop kick, jumping in the air and slamming his boot into Dr. Demented's face.

"On your knees, Doctor Demented! Get on your knees and beg for my forgiveness."

Dr. Demented lay there for what seemed like an eternity, but was actually just fifteen seconds. Slowly, as if every muscle in his body was crying out with pain, he pushed himself up to a kneeling position.

The crowd was going *insane*. Dr. Demented had *never* given up before. He had never even *lost* before. Professional wrestling history was happening before their eyes!

But suddenly, Dr. Demented shot out an arm and speared Sergeant America's right ankle. America went down and Dr. Demented leaped on him like a cat. He slammed his elbow into Sergeant America's midsection, pummeled him with punches, chops, and knees, and executed a drop toe-hold/face-lock combination that left Sergeant America stunned and helpless.

Sergeant America rolled out of the way, trying to get to the ropes. But Dr. Demented was too quick. He dragged the woozy Sergeant America back. Rather than go for the easy pin, he decided to inflict further punishment.

Dr. Demented picked America up, spun him upside down and hoisted him over his shoulders. Then, walking forward, he press slammed him, dropping him chest first to the mat.

Dr. Demented walked around Sergeant America's body, as if deciding whether he should hit him again or call an ambulance. He dragged the big man a few feet to one side, then ran to the corner of the ring and climbed up to the top rope.

"He's going to do it!" Jimmy marveled.

"Do what?" his dad asked.

"The Doctor Demented Death Drop," Jimmy replied. "It's his signature move."

Dr. Demented was on the top rope now, taunting the crowd. Sergeant America lay motionless on his back. Demented leaped off the rope, did two backward somersaults in the air, and then landed, chest first, on Sergeant America.

In ten minutes, it was over. As always, Dr. Demented was the winner. The referee slapped the mat three times with his hand, and Dr. Demented jumped up to do a little jig around Sergeant America's lifeless form. The crowd went crazy.

Dr. Demented climbed up on the top rope again and taunted the crowd some more, posing and showing off. Many of the fans threw things and screamed insults at him.

"I will *never* get down on my knees!" Dr. Demented repeated.

As he jumped out of the ring, Dr. Demented stumbled on the apron around the ropes and almost fell down. He grabbed Erica America's hand and together they ran out of the arena.

Sergeant America lay stretched out across the middle of the mat, eyes shut, seemingly unconscious. A siren was heard in the distance. Two men in emergency medical uniforms solemnly rolled Sergeant America's lifeless body onto a stretcher and carried him out of the ring.

A few minutes later, in the ready room, Sergeant America hopped off the stretcher.

"Nice job, Billy," Dr. Demented told Sergeant America, wrapping his thick arms around him.

"You were great, man," Sergeant America told Dr. Demented. "You gonna be okay?"

"I twisted my ankle coming off the rope," Dr. Demented replied, rubbing his leg.

"You gonna be okay for bowling on Wednesday?" asked Sergeant America.

"Yeah, I'll be fine," Dr. Demented replied. "Pick you up at nine."

The house lights in the Astrodome came on. Fifteen thousand contented fans gathered up their coats, fumbled for their car keys, and shuffled out the exits, just as if they had just attended a performance by the Houston Symphony orchestra.

Dr. Demented was already in the media room being interviewed by an AWF reporter.

"How did you feel," the reporter asked, "when the ref counted Sergeant America out?"

"Steve, I was thinking about how much fun it is to inflict extreme pain on another human being. I mean, what could be better than beating on someone's flesh and making them cry out in agony?"

"Well, thank you, Doctor Demented, for being the ruler of our pathetic world."

"Anytime, Steve."

3

Wesley Brown's Secret

"I'LL HAVE A CHOCOLATE MILKSHAKE," Wesley Brown told the waitress. After the Astrodome SkullCrush, Jimmy's dad drove the boys straight to the Sweet Dreams ice cream parlor in Humble, Texas. Jimmy and his dad each ordered a sundae.

Humble is a small town, about an hour from Houston. It's pronounced *umble*, without the H. Exxon started there a long time ago, under the name Humble Oil Company. There's still an old oil well there, right in the center of town.

Wesley Brown had a secret. He had never told his mother this secret. He had never told Jimmy, even though he was his best friend. He had never told anybody. In fact, he had never really admitted the secret to himself.

Wesley didn't really want a chocolate milkshake. He didn't particularly *like* chocolate milkshakes. But he had read in a magazine article that if you wanted to gain weight, you should eat bananas and drink chocolate milkshakes. Lots of them.

This was Wesley's secret: He hated the way he looked and was totally and completely obsessed with his physical appearance.

Most people looking at Wesley would think he was perfectly healthy and normal. He was. But at four feet eight inches, he was the shortest kid in the freshman class of Chester A. Nimitz High School—including the girls. He was the skinniest too, tipping the scale at barely eighty pounds.

It didn't seem to matter how much food Wesley ate, or *what* he ate. He never gained a pound. Once, during a checkup, his doctor explained that Wesley had high metabolism, whatever that meant. Other people, like his mother's friends, were actually *envious* of Wesley.

"I would give anything to be as skinny as you," these women would say, thinking they were giving him a compliment.

Wesley would have given anything to be heavier. He was disgusted by the way he looked. Sometimes, when his mother wasn't around, he would take off his shirt and go into her room to look at himself in her full-length mirror. Seeing the way his ribs poked through his skin, he imagined that he looked like one of those kids he saw in magazine ads asking people to send money to help feed starving children.

Looking in the mirror, he would flex his muscles the way bodybuilders did. Nothing. Barely a bump. To make things worse, Wesley had pimples that came and went for no reason, no matter how many creams or pads he rubbed against his face.

The waitress brought the milkshake to the table and Wesley downed it greedily. He fantasized that the shake was going directly from his mouth, down his throat, into his stomach, and then on to his major muscle groups, which would become bigger and stronger.

"Man, did you see when Demented picked Sergeant America up with one hand?" Jimmy marveled, spooning his sundae. Jimmy had *no* problem gaining weight. He seemed to put on pounds just by looking at food.

"He must weigh three hundred pounds, easy."

Wesley hadn't always been obsessed with weight. Up until seventh grade, he had never really thought about his weight at all. But then, after summer vacation that year, when he entered middle school, everything seemed different.

A lot of the boys he had known for years had gotten bigger and more muscular. A lot of the girls had gotten curvy and started wearing makeup. Suddenly, everybody was looking more like grownups than kids.

Except for Wesley. He still looked like a little boy.

"I wonder if Doctor Demented was ripped when he was our age," Wesley wondered.

"Bet he was a monster," Jimmy guessed.

It was the beginning of seventh grade when the teasing had begun at school. One of the bigger guys, Carl Campanella, started calling Wesley "Mouse." It caught on. Gradually Wesley lost his real name and became Mouse to a lot of the kids at school.

Nobody beat him up or anything. But he was conscious of the fact that anybody *could* beat him up if they wanted to. He thought about that every day.

"I bet Doctor Demented was the toughest kid in his high school," Wesley said.

Every day there were sad stories in magazines and on TV about high school girls who starved themselves and even threw up their food on purpose because they thought it would help them lose weight and look like fashion models or movie stars. But there were never any stories about the pressure on boys to look strong and "manly."

Wesley drained the last of his milkshake and thought about Sergeant America and Dr. Demented. That was what men were *supposed* to look like, he thought. You were supposed to have thick, well-defined muscles on your neck, shoulders, and arms. You were supposed to be "ripped."

You were supposed to have a "six-pack"—stomach muscles that looked like one of those six-packs of soda.

Wesley looked nothing like those guys. He didn't look like a man, he thought. He looked like a different species. An inferior species.

His solution to the problem was to hide his body. Even on the hottest day of the summer, he turned down invitations to go swimming. He didn't take a shower after gym class. He wore long sleeved shirts that were too big for him. He slouched when he walked or sat, as if he was trying to make himself invisible, or at least less noticeable.

One year Wesley's grandmother gave him a wristwatch for his birthday. Wesley tried it on, but even at the smallest size, the wristband slipped up and down his skinny arm. He put the watch in his drawer and never wore it.

Wesley never went to school dances. What girl would want to dance with him when she could dance with one of the big guys, the guys with muscles? When Jimmy tried to talk him into going to the seventh grade dance, Wesley said he wasn't feeling well that night.

Wesley glanced across the table at Jimmy and his dad slurping their sundaes. Both of them were badly overweight, but they didn't seem to care. Jimmy's nickname at school was "Blimpie," but he just laughed when people called him that.

If I had to choose between looking like me and looking like Jimmy, Wesley wondered, *who would I would rather be?* He decided he would rather be Jimmy. Jimmy was fat, but losing weight must be easier than gaining it. All you'd have to do would be to stop eating until you were normal. It would be simple.

At least Jimmy had muscles underneath there somewhere, Wesley reasoned. If he could get some of that fat out of the way, Jimmy would look pretty good. Wesley's body was hopeless.

Wesley kept this secret to himself. It was bad enough that he didn't look like a man. If he were to cry on somebody's shoulder about it, he would seem even less manly.

When they finished their ice cream, it was close to midnight. Mr. Erdman paid the check and drove Wesley home. Wesley thanked him for the evening as he got out of the car. He waved good-bye as the Erdmans pulled away from the curb.

Wesley was about to put his key in the lock when a car pulled into the driveway of the house on the corner of the street. Mr. Wheeler's house. Wesley recognized Mr. Wheeler's little red Mazda Miata sports car.

Landon Wheeler was the new gym teacher, a big man, and already one of the most popular teachers at Nimitz High School. He wasn't married and he didn't have any children. Mr. Wheeler was usually the only grown-up who would join in when kids in the neighborhood started playing stickball, football, or hockey in the street.

It was dark, but Wesley recognized Mr. Wheeler by the light on his porch. The teacher was carrying a gym bag and he appeared to be limping as he made his way slowly up the front steps. Wesley jogged over.

"You okay, Mr. Wheeler?" he asked.

"Yeah," he replied, grimacing. "I banged up my leg shooting hoops at the Y. What are you doing up so late?"

"I went to see pro wrestling at the Astrodome."

"Oh yeah? How was it?"

"Awesome! We saw Doctor Demented versus Sergeant America."

"Cool," Mr. Wheeler said. "Who won?"

"Doctor Demented. He always wins."

Wesley helped Mr. Wheeler up the final steps and then dashed home. He knew his mother was waiting up for him, and he didn't want her to worry.

4

Bonnie Brown's Secret

"WHERE WERE YOU?" WESLEY'S MOM ASKED nervously when Wesley opened the front door.

"Jimmy's dad took us out for ice cream afterward," Wesley replied. His dog, Mookie, yapped and jumped into his arms.

"You should have called."

"Sorry, Mom."

"Who was that man you helped up the steps?"

"Mr. Wheeler," Wesley replied, slightly annoyed that his mother had been peeking through the curtains at him. "He's the gym teacher at school. He just moved in last week."

In fact, Bonnie Brown, Wesley's mother, had been peeking through the front curtains for nearly an hour. A few more minutes and she would have called Jimmy's house. If there was no answer there, she was prepared to call the police.

"Did you have a good time?"

"It was unbelievable!" Wesley said excitedly. "You should have been there. Doctor Demented was flinging this guy around like he was a pizza. Can I go again sometime?"

Mrs. Brown sighed. It wasn't the answer she wanted to hear. Wesley had been begging her for permission to go see wrestling for months. She had hoped that allowing Wesley to go to Houston would get it out of his system and he would move on to more worthwhile interests. Playing a sport. A musical instrument. A hobby. Anything but professional wrestling.

Like Wesley, Bonnie Brown had a secret that she hadn't told anyone. Not even Wesley. The secret was this—Wesley's father, her ex-husband, had been physically abusive.

They had been high school sweethearts growing up in Salem, Massachusetts. She had been the drum majorette, a blond-haired, blue-eyed beauty. At thirty-three years old, she was still a very pretty woman.

Wesley's father had been captain of the high school wrestling team. Cheering him on, Bonnie learned a lot about the sport. She could name all the takedowns, counters, escapes, reversals, and so on. He and Bonnie were meant for each other, everyone thought at the time.

Only later, in a marriage counselor's office, would they admit the attraction was only physical. He liked the shape of her upper torso. She liked the shape of his lower abdominals. Too bad their bodies couldn't get married and leave their minds out of it.

Things got bad almost as soon as the honeymoon was over. He didn't get the wrestling scholarship he had hoped for, and didn't want to go to college without one. She continued with her schooling, earned a degree in music education, and eventually got a job as a music teacher.

He got a job working for a roofing company. He had no skills and didn't want to learn any. When he finally realized that nobody cared about the wrestling trophies he had won in high school, he started getting depressed and coming home late.

His "six-pack" that she found so attractive disappeared under a layer of fat, because he drank too many six-packs. When she complained about his drinking one day, he hit her with an open fist.

When she was pregnant, he couldn't make the time to attend childbirth classes or read any books on child rearing. She decided that if he hit her in front of the baby, she would leave him.

He did, and she did. She got a restraining order that made it illegal for him to come within three hundred feet of her or baby Wesley. It wasn't necessary. He moved to Florida and that was that.

He didn't ask for custody of Wesley or visitation rights. She didn't ask for child support payments.

She knew he couldn't support himself, much less a child.

Wesley never knew any of this about his father. All his mother told him was that her marriage didn't work out, and that his father moved away when he was a baby. It was the truth, if not the whole truth. She decided that she would tell him the entire story someday, if he asked. So far, he hadn't.

Bonnie Brown involuntarily touched her left cheek, the cheek where her husband used to smack her. She still remembered very clearly what it felt like to be hit by an angry man. She didn't like the idea of wrestling one bit.

She worried constantly about Wesley. When he was younger, he was such a sweet, gentle little boy. He used to take insects and plants and examine them under a microscope or photograph them. She still had some of his pictures hanging on the walls of the kitchen. Back then, he seemed to be the exact opposite of his father.

In the last year or two, though, a change had come over Wesley. He didn't seem to care about anything meaningful. His grades had slipped. He had become very sensitive, getting angry at the least little thing. All he wanted to do was watch wrestling on TV, listen to angry music, and play computer games that had warning labels on the box.

Her worst fear was that Wesley would turn out to be a violent man like his father. Wesley was such a little guy. How would he defend himself if he got into trouble?

"I'm not sure if I want you to go see wrestling again," she told Wesley.

"Oh man, why not?"

"You know why. It's violent."

"It's fake violence, Mom!" Wesley protested. "Nobody's really getting hurt!"

"Fake violence leads to real violence," his mother replied. "People imitate what they see."

"They do not!"

Wesley stamped his feet and stormed upstairs, slamming the door behind him. He'd had this debate with his mother before. There was no convincing her that wrestling was just harmless fun. He couldn't understand why it was such a big issue with her. But then, he didn't know what she had lived through with his father.

Wesley flipped off the light in his room and clicked on his flashlight. He reached under his mattress and pulled out a magazine. He had bought it at the supermarket without telling his mother, or anyone else.

The name of the magazine was *Totally Ripped*. Wesley balanced the flashlight on his shoulder and flipped through the pages. There were 340 of them, most of them advertisements.

Totally Ripped was the best-selling magazine about bodybuilding. On virtually every page was a man—or occasionally a woman—with ridiculously enormous muscles posing to make those muscles look as pumped up as possible.

The bodybuilders on the pages of *Totally Ripped* had veins popping through their chest and arms and legs like road maps. Their bodies looked like movable plastic action figure toys.

Usually, the guy in the photos was lifting a dumbbell with one hand and had an intense look on his face, like he was in serious pain. In some of the photos, the guy was being hugged by a beautiful girl wearing a bikini. The message was obvious: If you had big muscles like this guy, beautiful girls would like you, too.

Wesley scanned the ads. There were one or two ads for exercise equipment, but most of them were for pills you could take that would help you get bigger muscles.

EAT NAILS FOR BREAKFAST . . . WHY BE A BIRD-CHESTED WEAKLING? . . . GAIN TEN POUNDS IN MINUTES . . . THE QUICKEST ROUTE TO EXPLOSIVE MUSCLE MASS . . . RIPPED ABS IN 28 DAYS . . . ANYTHING STRONGER IS ILLEGAL! . . . GROWTH HORMONE—IT GROWS MUSCLES . . . LEGAL STEROL COMPLEX . . .

It went on and on. Wesley stopped at an ad for something called "Creatine Cocktail." On the left was a "before" photo of a scrawny little guy with a body that looked a lot like his. On the right was an "after" photo that had been taken eight weeks later. In the after photo, the same guy had huge popping muscles, a pretty girl on his arm, and a big smile on his face.

It *looked* like the same guy, anyway. The photo could have been retouched to put the skinny guy's face on a muscular guy's body. Wesley couldn't tell for sure.

Maybe all these pills are bogus, Wesley thought. *Maybe it's like when doctors give patients a sugar pill and tell them it's medicine so they'll convince themselves to get better.* The muscle-building pills could be fake the same way he knew professional wrestling was fake.

On the other hand though, maybe the stuff *worked*. Wesley had heard kids in the locker room after gym class talking about creatine and how big it made their muscles. Sometimes it was hard to tell what was real and what was fake.

Wesley fell asleep with his head on the magazine.

5

Landon Wheeler's Secret

WESLEY BROWN DIDN'T NEED AN ALARM clock to wake up in the morning. He had Mookie. Every morning at almost exactly seven o'clock, Mookie would come into Wesley's room, leap on his bed, and start licking Wesley's ears. Mookie didn't understand that on weekends human beings stayed up later and then slept later in the morning.

It was Sunday morning, the day after the wrestling match. Wearily, Wesley pulled on some sweats and grabbed Mookie's leash. Still half asleep, he shuffled outside with Mookie straining at the leash to run ahead.

Usually, Mookie would head left down the street. But this day he dashed right. Wesley followed. Except for a few similarly sleep-deprived dog walkers, there wasn't anybody out this early. Wesley let Mookie wander wherever his nose took him. He didn't have to get to school, so he let Mookie have a longer walk than usual.

After finding a suitable spot to do his business, Mookie was ready to move on. Wesley used the plastic bag the newspaper had been wrapped in to pick up Mookie's mess.

Mookie stopped to sniff the flowers in front of Mr. Wheeler's house. Wesley remembered helping Mr. Wheeler up the steps the previous night and wondered if his ankle was better.

"Uh!"

It was a grunt. Or maybe a moan. Either a grunt or a moan or a groan came out of Mr. Wheeler's house. Wesley stopped and listened more carefully.

"Uh!"

Another one. Definitely a groan. *The poor guy must be in a lot of pain*, Wesley thought. Mr. Wheeler's red sports car was still parked in the driveway. There was a newspaper on the front lawn. Wesley brought it up the steps in case Mr. Wheeler wasn't able to walk outside to get it.

"Uh!"

There it was again. It seemed to be coming from inside the garage. Wesley was getting worried now. He thought about running home to call 911.

"Mr. Wheeler?" he called out, walking around the house to the garage with Mookie. "Are you okay?"

"Uh!"

Something was definitely wrong with Mr. Wheeler. He might have fallen and couldn't get up. Hurriedly, Wesley reached down for the handle of the garage door and used all his strength to yank it up.

Mr. Wheeler was lying on a bench, holding a barbell over his head with a stack of fat black weights on each side of the bar. The garage had been turned into a little gym, with weights and weight machines all around. Mr. Wheeler rested the barbell on a rack above his head and took off the headphones he had been wearing.

"G'morning, Wesley!" Mr. Wheeler said cheerfully.

In his gym shorts and T-shirt, Mr. Wheeler looked a lot bigger than he did when he was dressed up at school. Wesley always noticed other people's muscles, and the muscles in Mr. Wheeler's arms and legs strained against his clothing.

"I'm sorry!" Wesley exclaimed. "I didn't know you were busy."

"I'm done," Mr. Wheeler replied. "Come on in."

"Here's your newspaper," Wesley said. "I'll come back another time."

"I'm baking muffins," Mr. Wheeler said. "They'll be out of the oven in a few minutes."

"Well . . ." Wesley was a sucker for a good muffin.

Mr. Wheeler got up off the bench gingerly and led Wesley and Mookie through a door that went directly from the garage into his kitchen. He was still limping. Classical music was playing on the stereo.

"How's your ankle?" Wesley asked.

"Getting better."

Mr. Wheeler took the muffins out of the oven and put one on a plate for each of them. Wesley took a bite and moaned with delight.

"All natural," Mr. Wheeler revealed. "No artificial ingredients. No preservatives. Chock full of good stuff."

"It's delicious," Wesley added, his mouth full of muffin.

"How about a glass of milk?" Mr. Wheeler asked.

"No thanks."

"Calcium, protein, and vitamin D," Mr. Wheeler said. "Best fuel in the world for a growing body."

"Well, okay."

While Mr. Wheeler was pouring the milk and getting another muffin, Wesley let Mookie off his leash. The dog sniffed around Mr. Wheeler's kitchen, then went to sniff the living room.

There, Mookie came upon a gym bag, the same gym bag Mr. Wheeler had been carrying up the steps the night before. The zipper wasn't closed all the way, and Mookie stuck his head in the opening.

There was something in the gym bag that

caught Mookie's interest. And when Mookie was interested in something, there was nothing stopping him.

The little dog pulled and poked with his teeth and paws until he was able to pull out the object of his desire. It was black, and made of leather. He picked it up with his teeth and carried it into the kitchen. Mookie dropped the black leather thing at Wesley's feet. A little trophy for his master.

"One eight ounce cup of milk provides eight grams of protein," Mr. Wheeler was telling Wesley as he washed the muffin tin at the sink. "When I was a kid, I drank milk all day long. We had to. Nowadays, kids hardly drink any milk. They have soda machines in schools. Can you believe that? Soda machines in school? Do you know how many grams of sugar are in a single can of soda? Forty-one grams."

While Mr. Wheeler was talking, Wesley put his second muffin down and picked up the black thing Mookie had brought him. Putting his hand in the bigger hole, he could see it was about the shape of a person's head, and there were holes for two eyes, a nose, and a mouth.

"What did you find, boy?" Wesley asked Mookie.

At the sink, Mr. Wheeler turned around. When he saw what Wesley was holding, his jaw dropped open.

Wesley saw the expression on Mr. Wheeler's face. He looked at the black leather mask in his hand. He thought about Mr. Wheeler limping. He thought about last night. He looked at the muscles on Mr. Wheeler's arms. And he came to a conclusion, the only conclusion that made any sense at all.

"You're Doctor Demented!"

6

The Secret Life of
Dr. Demented

WESLEY STARED AT MR. WHEELER FOR A
second or two, and Mr. Wheeler stared back at
him. Neither one was sure what to do next.

Wesley couldn't believe what he had just discovered. Mr. Wheeler, the friendly guy down the
street who taught gym at Nimitz High, led a secret
life as Dr. Demented, the meanest, cruelest, and
most violent man in the AWF.

Wesley made the first move.

"Let's go, Mookie!" he yelled, leaping off the
kitchen chair.

Wesley grabbed the leash and snatched up
Mookie in the same motion. He dashed out of Mr.
Wheeler's kitchen, desperately searching for the
front door. He ran into the living room. Mookie,
who had no idea what all the fuss was about,
started barking loudly.

"Wesley, wait!" hollered Mr. Wheeler.

He dropped the muffin pan he had been scrubbing into the sink and took off after Wesley. The injury to his ankle made it difficult for him to move very well. With every step, he felt a jab of pain shoot up his right leg. Mr. Wheeler hobbled out of the kitchen.

"Wesley, you don't understand!" he shouted.

Landon Wheeler was furious at himself. For the past five years, he hadn't told anyone in the "real world" that he moonlighted as a professional wrestler. Not even his own mother knew the truth. And now, his secret had been discovered— by a *dog*.

Wesley fumbled frantically with the deadbolt lock on Mr. Wheeler's front door, turning the knob left and right in a frantic attempt to get the door open. With Mookie curled up on his arm, he was having trouble with the lock.

He had to get out of there. Even if wrestling was fake, Wesley knew that Dr. Demented was capable of hurting a person really badly if he wanted to. Having seen what Dr. Demented did to Sergeant America in the ring the night before, there was no telling what he might to do *him*.

Finally the deadbolt clicked the right way and Wesley yanked the door open. Mr. Wheeler was only halfway across the living room. There was nothing he could do to stop Wesley from running out of his house.

"Wesley! I'm *not* Doctor Demented!"

Wesley stopped in the doorway, panting. *If he's not Doctor Demented*, Wesley thought, *then why does he have Doctor Demented's mask in his house? And why is he limping? And why, now that I notice it, does he have muscles big enough to pulverize a minivan?*

"Please," Mr. Wheeler said softly. "Please don't leave."

The voice was so gentle. Wesley turned around and came back inside the living room. Mookie jumped out of his arms and scampered away. Mr. Wheeler sat on the couch heavily, grunting as he elevated his sore leg on the coffee table. He had known all along that eventually someone would discover he was Dr. Demented. Now it had happened.

"Are you going to . . . kill me?" Wesley asked meekly, taking a seat.

"Kill you?" Mr. Wheeler chuckled. "What for?"

"For finding out your secret," Wesley replied. "So I can't tell anyone."

"I'm not Doctor Demented, Wesley," Mr. Wheeler explained. "Doctor Demented is just a *role* I play. You understand that, don't you?"

Wesley nodded. He would have agreed with anything Mr. Wheeler said. Anything to avoid getting hurt.

"You've seen shows like *ER* on TV, right, Wesley? You realize that they're not real doctors and the patients aren't real patients, don't you?

They're just actors playing doctors and patients. It's the same with me. I play this character called Doctor Demented. I'm not mean out of the ring. And the guy who plays Sergeant America is a nice guy. But he's not any nicer than I am, and I love my country just as much as he does. You see?"

"So you didn't steal Sergeant America's wife?" Wesley asked.

Mr. Wheeler laughed. "He's not even married. She was an actress playing his wife."

Wesley's breathing finally returned to normal. Mr. Wheeler sighed. Both of them relaxed a little.

"It's almost a relief knowing that somebody else knows my secret," Mr. Wheeler said. "I've kept it hidden for a long time."

Mr. Wheeler proceeded to tell Wesley the story of how he went from being normal Landon Wheeler to evil Dr. Demented.

He had been on his high school and college wrestling teams, he explained. He was good, so good that he was expected to make the U.S. Olympic team his senior year at UCLA. In the finals though, he was beaten by a guy from Michigan State.

Mr. Wheeler was devastated by the loss, and was so upset that he didn't even watch the Olympics on television. He gave up wrestling and went back to school to get a degree to teach physical education.

During his first year of teaching, Mr. Wheeler

got a call one day from an AWF promoter who had seen him wrestle in college. The promoter was looking for new faces and asked Landon if he might be interested in giving professional wrestling a try.

At first Mr. Wheeler turned the guy down flat. He was a wrestler, not a clown. He didn't want to play some silly character and scream dumb things into a microphone to get a crowd riled up. He didn't want to twirl opponents over his head, fling them out of the ring, or do any of those other ridiculous show-off moves professional wrestlers have to do. He was a pure wrestler, an *amateur* wrestler.

Plus, he didn't want guys hitting him over the head with baseball bats or metal folding chairs.

Besides, Mr. Wheeler told the promoter, he had a career now. The board of education would never approve of a gym teacher who beat up guys—and sometimes women—for the amusement of an audience.

But the promoter was persuasive. He suggested that Mr. Wheeler could wear a mask in the ring, so nobody would know his true identity. Furthermore, he offered a starting salary of a thousand dollars for each match. If Mr. Wheeler's character caught on with the fans and he became a star, the promoter promised, he could earn much more than that.

That got Landon Wheeler thinking. A thousand

dollars for a few hours of work one night a week! That was a lot more money than he earned teaching gym. He could certainly use the money. There was this red sports car he had his eye on.

He had to admit, pretending to beat guys up sounded a lot easier than grading papers, preparing lesson plans, and dealing with high school students.

And that's how Landon Wheeler became Dr. Demented.

"You believe me, don't you?" Mr. Wheeler asked when he'd finished telling the story.

Wesley had been sitting there, drinking it all in. Mr. Wheeler certainly sounded like he was telling the truth. His story made sense, certainly more sense than AWF's version of Dr. Demented's history. According to them, Dr. Demented was raised by wolves in Death Valley, Nevada, and crawled on his hands and knees through the desert to California, where he escaped from a mental institution by strangling all the guards with barbed wire.

"I believe you," Wesley said. "But why don't you play a good guy?"

"The AWF controls a professional wrestler's character, not the wrestler," Mr. Wheeler explained. "We win matches when they tell us to win. We job when they tell us to job. It's in our contract."

"Job?" Wesley asked.

"Lose," Mr. Wheeler replied.

Wesley was well aware that the outcome of professional wrestling matches was predetermined. Only a fool believed the fights were real.

"Whatever happened to that guy who beat you out of a spot on the Olympic team?" Wesley asked. "Did he win a medal?"

"Nah. He got beaten in the first round. I hear he turned pro, too. He lives somewhere in California and wrestles under the name of Terminator or something like that."

Wesley shook his head in wonder. Last night he had been watching a masked maniac go berserk and nearly tear a guy limb from limb. Now he was sitting in the living room of the maniac, who turned out to be his gym teacher and neighbor. And who happened to bake fantastic muffins. Strange world.

For the first time, Wesley took his eyes off Mr. Wheeler and looked around the room. There were abstract paintings on the walls, lots of bookshelves, and some African masks. There was nothing to indicate that Mr. Wheeler was a professional wrestler. It could have been anybody's house.

On the coffee table was a thick book titled *Gray's Anatomy*. Wesley picked it up and leafed through the pages. They were filled with pictures of hearts, lungs, and other body parts.

"I'm studying for the MCAT," Mr. Wheeler explained. "Medical College Achievement Test."

"What's that?"

"It's a test you have to take to get into medical school."

"You want to be a doctor?" Wesley asked.

"A pediatrician," Mr. Wheeler replied. "I always liked kids. My goal is to wrestle until I've saved two hundred thousand dollars. Then I'm going to take four years off from teaching and go to med school full time."

"I guess as a doctor you won't be calling yourself Doctor Demented," Wesley joked.

They both laughed. Wesley was no longer afraid that Mr. Wheeler was going to do him bodily harm. It was kind of cool, he decided, to live down the street from Dr. Demented.

"Is it true that you once ripped a guy's ear off and ate it?" Wesley asked.

"We faked that," Mr. Wheeler chuckled. "A little dough, a little tomato sauce. It didn't taste bad, actually. If we had a little cheese, it would have made a pretty good pizza."

Mookie came running back in and Wesley put the leash on him. If he didn't get back home soon, he knew his mom would start worrying.

"Wait until I tell everybody at school that I live down the street from Doctor Demented!" he marveled.

Mr. Wheeler stood up and put his thick hand over the door so it couldn't be opened. Then he put his face very close to Wesley's.

"Don't tell anyone," he said, almost menacingly.

"Even my mother?"

"Even your mother!"

"Uh, sure," Wesley stammered. "Why not?"

"Do you know what would happen to me if word got out that I was Doctor Demented?" Mr. Wheeler continued. "I would lose my job at school. People might want me out of this neighborhood. And I would never get into medical school."

"Why not?"

"Doctors are supposed to *stop* pain," Mr. Wheeler said, "not start it."

"I won't tell anyone," Wesley promised.

"Thank you," Mr. Wheeler replied. "I appreciate it."

Wesley gave a pull on Mookie's leash and Mr. Wheeler opened the front door. On the porch, Wesley stopped and turned around as if he had forgotten something.

"Thanks for the muffins."

7

Twenty Questions

ALL MORNING LONG WESLEY FOUND IT hard to hide the goofy grin on his face. He still couldn't get over the fact that Mr. Wheeler down the street—his own gym teacher—was Dr. Demented, the most feared man in the AWF. And he, Wesley Brown, was the only kid who knew the secret.

Professional wrestlers have to live *somewhere*, he reasoned. Why not on his street? *Doctor Demented . . . er, Mr. Wheeler, probably likes the idea of living in a quiet suburban neighborhood as much as anybody.*

Jimmy Erdman stopped by after lunch, figuring Wesley might want to play computer games or something.

"Are you okay?" Jimmy asked almost as soon as Wesley opened the door.

"Yeah, why?"

"Something's going on."

"What makes you say that?"

"You've got this weird look on your face. Like you're in shock or something. What is it?"

"I'm in shock."

"What happened?"

"I can't tell you."

"Why not?"

"I'm sworn to secrecy."

"Oh come on, Wesley. You can tell me. What's the big deal?"

"I'm sorry, Jimmy. I just can't."

"Does anybody else know the secret?"

"No. Only the person who told me."

"Come on, Wes. I won't tell anybody."

"I promised I'd keep it a secret."

"But I'm your best friend."

"I just can't tell you."

"It must be something really incredible."

"It is," Wesley replied with a little smile. "It's like the most amazing thing in the world."

"Oh, c'mon, please tell me?"

"No."

"How about if I guess?"

"You'll never guess. Not in a million years."

"Lemme try."

"No."

"How about we play twenty questions?"

"What's that?"

"You know," Jimmy explained, "I ask you a series of yes or no questions. If I haven't figured out the big secret in twenty questions, I lose. I'll never bother you about it again."

Wesley thought it over. He was pretty much of a whiz at math, but Jimmy was a genius at *everything*. He got straight A's in school and he never even had to study. He knew things that nobody else knew, like what part of the world East Timor was in. But there was no way Jimmy was going to guess that Mr. Wheeler was Dr. Demented. Not if he asked a *million* questions. It was impossible.

"Okay," Wesley agreed. "Twenty questions. And no more."

"You can't back out in the middle, you understand?" Jimmy insisted.

"I won't."

"Deal," the two boys said as they shook on it.

"Now let me get this straight," Jimmy said slowly. "There is some really incredible secret, and you and somebody else are the only ones who know it. Right?"

"Is that your first question?"

"Yes," Jimmy replied. "I just want to make sure we're clear on everything."

"We're clear."

"Good. Now tell me, does this big secret have anything to do with you?"

"No. That's two questions down."

Jimmy rubbed his hands together and began pacing the room. "Does the secret have anything to do with somebody at school?"

"Yes."

"Aha! Now we're getting somewhere."

Wesley was already getting the feeling that he never should have agreed to play twenty questions with Jimmy. Jimmy was just too sharp. If he guessed the secret and Mr. Wheeler found out about it, there would be big trouble.

"So . . ." continued Jimmy. "The big secret involves somebody at school."

"You've used three of your twenty questions."

"Is it a student?"

"No. Four questions."

"Okay. So it's one of the teachers or staff members. Is it Principal Wilson?"

"No. That's five."

"Mrs. Sammut?" Mrs. Sammut was their homeroom teacher.

"No. That's six."

"Hmmmm." Jimmy realized that he could use up all his twenty questions just going through names to find out who the secret was about. Then he wouldn't have any questions left to find out what the secret was. He had to try a different strategy.

"Is it a female?"

"No. That's seven."

"So it's one of the *male* teachers!" Jimmy announced proudly. "There aren't that many male teachers at our school, and you only know a few of them. Is it Mr. Foster?"

"No. That's eight."

"Mr. Wheeler?"

Wesley moaned. What a fool he had been to agree to play this stupid game with Jimmy.

"Look, you've got to go home," Wesley grumbled. "I think my mom needs me to do some chores."

"Aha! It's Mr. Wheeler!" Jimmy exclaimed. "So you have this incredible secret that you claim nobody else knows, and it involves Mr. Wheeler, the gym teacher. How many questions do I have left?"

"Is that one of your questions?"

"No, if I ask you how many questions I have left, it doesn't count as a question."

"You asked nine questions, so you have eleven left."

"Mr. Wheeler. Mr. Wheeler," Jimmy continued to pace back and forth, his hands behind his back, as he thought out loud. "There is some truly amazing fact that you have somehow figured out about Mr. Wheeler that nobody else knows. Maybe he's a mass murderer or something . . ."

"Is that a question?"

"No, I'm just thinking to myself. He probably isn't a criminal or you would have called the police. Maybe Mr. Wheeler did some really tremendous thing like find a cure for diabetes. But if that were true, he would be proud of it and wouldn't swear you to secrecy. I suspect it's something that he's kind of ashamed of. Something unusual about him he would prefer that people didn't know."

"Time's up," Wesley said hopefully.

"Twenty questions is like baseball," Jimmy explained. "No time limit. Now let me think. Mr. Wheeler could wear a toupee or something, but that wouldn't be such a big deal. Maybe he dug up something amazing in his backyard."

Jimmy looked at Wesley to see if he would react. He didn't, so Jimmy pressed on.

"Maybe he's the brother of somebody really famous," Jimmy tossed out. "Or maybe he's got a secret life or something."

Wesley shook his head sadly. Jimmy was getting too close. He didn't like it. Jimmy picked up on Wesley's reaction.

"Does Mr. Wheeler have a secret life?"

"Yes," Wesley moaned, vowing to hide his thoughts better. "That's ten questions."

"So Mr. Wheeler has a secret life, eh? A secret identity, like Superman. What could it be? Let me think. What kind of a secret stuff could a gym teacher be doing in his spare time?"

"Yes or no questions only."

"I'm just thinking to myself," Jimmy continued. "It has to be something he does after school or on weekends. It's not likely that he's a famous singer or anything. His voice is too gruff. He might be an actor. But if he was an actor, I would probably recognize his face. His secret life has to involve something where people can't see his face."

Jimmy was like a bloodhound tracking down an escaped convict. Wesley thought that maybe he should start lying. He could throw Jimmy off the trail with a few simple no's that were really yes's or yes's that were really no's. But if he lied, he would have to come up with a phony secret about Mr. Wheeler. That could cause even more problems.

"Mr. Wheeler is a pretty big guy, and he teaches gym," Jimmy mused. "Is he some kind of an athlete on the side?"

"You're good," groaned Wesley. "Real good. That's eleven."

"I know I am. You told me I wouldn't be able to guess this amazing secret in a million years. But with eleven simple questions, I have determined that our gym teacher Mr. Wheeler has a secret life as a professional athlete. Now I have to determine what sport he plays."

"I think we should stop right here," Wesley said. "You won the game."

"Not yet. I haven't figured out the amazing secret yet. Is he a football player?"

"No. Twelve questions."

"Hockey player?"

"No. That's thirteen."

"Is it baseball?"

"No. Fourteen." Wesley began to feel some hope. Jimmy was running out of questions.

"It can't be basketball because Mr. Wheeler isn't tall enough," Jimmy said. "Is it boxing? Is he a boxer?"

"No. Fifteen."

Jimmy realized he had been off on another wild-goose chase, wasting his valuable questions. If Mr. Wheeler had played one of the major sports, everybody would know it. They'd see his face on TV. And because he worked five days a week at school, he wouldn't have time to train and travel around the country with a sports team. He only had five questions left.

Jimmy tried to think of a game that was played at night or on weekends with athletes who wore something that covered their faces. Fencing? Jai alai?

That's when it hit him. Jimmy's eyes opened wide as he asked question number sixteen.

"Is Mr. Wheeler . . . a professional wrestler?"

Wesley couldn't bring himself to respond. All he could think of was the beating Mr. Wheeler was going to give him when the teacher found out he had not kept the secret.

"You're kidding, right?" Jimmy asked, laughing. "Mr. Wheeler, a wrestler? This was all a big joke, right?"

"Uh, yeah," Wesley said, brightening. "It was all a big joke. Ha ha. Pretty funny, huh?"

"You're *not* kidding! Mr. Wheeler *is* a professional wrestler!"

"He's gonna kill me," Wesley said glumly. "He's gonna absolutely kill me."

"How did you find out that Mr. Wheeler was a professional wrestler?"

"It's a long story. Mookie pulled his costume out of a gym bag."

"That's not such a long story," Jimmy commented. "So what's the costume? Which wrestler is he?"

"I'm not telling."

"Oh, come on. I got this far on my own."

"I promised I wouldn't tell."

"Fine. I still have four questions left. Is he The Beast?"

"No."

"Is he Dave Adams, the Chainsaw Maniac?"

"No."

"Eric the Insane Viking?"

"No. That's nineteen."

Jimmy scrunched up his eyes and ran every professional wrestler who wore a mask through his head. He eliminated all the African-Americans, because Mr. Wheeler wasn't black. He eliminated the ones who had tattoos on their arms, because Mr. Wheeler didn't have any.

Slowly, a grin spread across Jimmy's face. There was only one wrestler left. It had to be. It couldn't be, but it had to be.

"Mr. Wheeler is—" Jimmy drew the words out to torture Wesley just a little longer—"Doctor Demented?"

Wesley hung his head.

"Game. Set. Match. Checkmate!" announced Jimmy triumphantly. "Hey, am I good, or what?"

8

Boys Will Be Jerks

"HE'S GONNA KILL ME," WESLEY SAID FOR the fourth time after Jimmy figured out that Mr. Wheeler led a secret life as Dr. Demented. "He's gonna kill me."

"He's not gonna kill you," Jimmy assured his friend. "He'll probably just break your arms and legs."

"Go ahead and make jokes," Wesley complained. "I promised Mr. Wheeler I wouldn't tell anybody he was Doctor Demented, and an hour later I told you."

"You didn't tell me. I guessed."

"Same difference," Wesley muttered. "You know the secret now."

"Yeah, but unlike you, I can keep a secret," Jimmy said.

"You better, Jimmy. I swear, if you breathe a word of this to anybody, I'll never speak to you again."

*   *   *

Jimmy Erdman proved to be a man of his word. In homeroom the next morning, he didn't say a word to anybody about Mr. Wheeler. He kept his mouth shut during lunch, too, even when some of the boys started talking about what Dr. Demented had done to Sergeant America on Saturday night. When Mr. Wheeler walked into the gym for phys ed the last period of the day (limping slightly), all Jimmy did was throw Wesley a wink.

Wesley felt like gym class was The Twilight Zone. While Mr. Wheeler was leading the boys through their stretching, sit-ups, and sprints, all Wesley could think about was Dr. Demented in that evil black mask. When Mr. Wheeler sat all the boys down on the gym floor and talked about the importance of eating lots of protein-rich foods, all Wesley could think about was Dr. Demented holding Sergeant America over his head and slamming him down on the mat like a cheap toy. Wesley kept trying to make eye contact with Mr. Wheeler, but the gym teacher didn't look in his direction.

Toward the end of the period, Mr. Wheeler lowered two thick ropes that were attached to the ceiling of the gym. The dreaded ropes. Wesley and Jimmy moved to the back of the group of boys.

Mr. Wheeler split the class in two groups and had the boys line up in front of the ropes. Two by two, they would race to see who could get to the top and ring the bell on the gym ceiling.

Jimmy and Wesley went to the end of one line. Maybe, with some luck, Wesley figured, the period would come to an end before it would be his turn to climb the rope. Or maybe an asteroid would hit the school, he hoped, and the rest of gym class would be canceled.

Mr. Wheeler blew his whistle and the first two boys started climbing furiously—Carl Campanella and Joey O'Neil. Those two big jocks were always first in line. Carl reached the top just before Joey. The next two boys both made it to the top, too. In the third group, one of the boys struggled and only made it halfway up before sliding down. The next two boys both made it to the top.

Jimmy was next. When Mr. Wheeler blew his whistle, the boy at the other rope climbed effortlessly and rang the bell. Jimmy reached up and pulled on the rope. He couldn't lift his weight off the ground. A few of the boys started giggling.

"Ever try pickin' up an elephant?" somebody whispered too loudly.

"Just pretend there's a chocolate cake at the top!" somebody cracked.

After one more try, Jimmy managed to get his body about a foot off the ground. Exhausted, he let go of the rope. While the other boys laughed and cheered, Jimmy smiled and took a deep bow as if to acknowledge their applause.

Wesley watched, envious, wishing he could laugh it off when kids made fun of him like that.

He positioned himself in front of the rope and got ready. When Mr. Wheeler blew his whistle, Wesley grabbed the rope and pulled.

He did better than Jimmy. Wesley was able to lift his slender body up and wrap his legs around the rope so he wouldn't slip down. He made it five feet or so up before the strain on his shoulders and arms was unbearable.

Wesley struggled to come down without getting rope burns on his hands. Nobody was laughing at him out loud, but he thought he heard some snickering from a few of the jocks. He didn't look at anybody.

When the bell rang, Mr. Wheeler dismissed the class and asked Wesley to come into his office.

"Don't feel bad about the ropes," he said. "Lots of boys can't get as high as you did."

"I know," Wesley said, not entirely convinced.

"Wesley, I just wanted you to know that I'm not going to treat you any differently than anybody else in the class," Mr. Wheeler told him. "At school, I'm just going to be boring Mr. Wheeler. I don't feel that what you found out yesterday should change anything that goes on here. Do you?"

"No, Mr. Wheeler."

"I'm glad we're in agreement. Thanks, Wesley."

By the time Wesley went to change out of his gym clothes, the locker room was empty. He liked that. It meant he wouldn't have to take his shirt off in front of the other guys. He was almost finished dressing when he realized his street shoes weren't with the rest of his stuff.

Wesley looked under all the benches and on top of the locker in case he had put his shoes there or somebody moved them. They were gone.

Brand new shoes. That was his first thought. His mom would go crazy when she found out he had lost them. Somebody must have stolen them. But who steals a pair of shoes?

Then Wesley noticed a small piece of paper at the bottom of his locker. He opened it up and this is what it said. . . .

MOUSE, YOUR SHOES ARE OUTSIDE.

Wesley rushed to put his sneakers back on, and ran out the back exit of the gym. Five or six boys were sitting out there smoking cigarettes. Wesley recognized Carl Campanella and Joey O'Neil. When they saw Wesley open the door, they stopped talking and looked at him.

"Where are my shoes?" Wesley demanded.

"How about a hello?" asked Carl, and a few of the boys snickered.

"Where did you put my shoes?" Wesley asked more insistently.

"How should we know where your shoes are?" one of the boys said.

Wesley noticed the boy who said that glance upward. Wesley looked up and saw his shoes—the laces tied together and both shoes dangling from the telephone line above the school.

Wesley clenched his hand into a fist. He knew he couldn't fight them. Even if it was one on one, the smallest of them was bigger than he was.

"Those your shoes?" one of the boys asked. "What are they doin' up there?" The other boys giggled.

"Who wrote the note?" Wesley demanded.

"What note?"

"You know what note!"

"We don't know what you're talking about, Mouse," Carl said, flicking away his cigarette. "Come on, let's get out of here. This guy is psycho. There's no telling what he might do."

Carl, Joey, and their friends walked away, laughing.

Wesley's heart was beating furiously. He looked up at the shoes hanging from the wire. He couldn't climb up there. He couldn't throw anything at them and knock them down. The shoes were going to be up there for a long time. He sat down on the curb and tried to figure out what he should do next.

If he told his mother what happened, she would be mad, big time. She had paid something like fifty dollars for those shoes just a week earlier. He only had about twenty-five dollars in his bank at home. He was stuck. He felt a tear in his eye and wiped it away. All he needed was for somebody to see him crying.

A few cars went by, and then a little red sports car pulled up to the curb. Wesley recognized Mr. Wheeler's Miata right away.

"What's up?" he asked Wesley.

"That," Wesley said, pointing to the telephone line.

Mr. Wheeler saw the shoes. He didn't need an explanation for what had happened.

"Who did it?" he asked.

"A bunch of guys," Wesley replied. "I'm not sure which one."

"Hop in," Mr. Wheeler said, flipping open the passenger door.

"Where are we going?"

"You'll see."

9

Jimmy Erdman's Secret

DOCTOR DEMENTED IS TAKING ME SHOP-ping for shoes.

Wesley couldn't get this strange thought out of his mind. In fact, Mr. Wheeler not only drove him to a shoe store, he also helped him find the exact same style of shoes his mother had bought him. He even made sure they fit perfectly, and had the salesman throw in an extra set of laces.

Then, to Wesley's astonishment, Mr. Wheeler pulled out his credit card and paid for the shoes with his own money. No matter how many times Wesley offered to pay him back, Mr. Wheeler refused to take any money.

"You saved my life," Wesley said. "I won't have to tell my mom what happened."

"You keep my secret and I'll keep yours."

Wesley felt awful. He couldn't bring himself to tell Mr. Wheeler that he had already shared the secret of Dr. Demented with his friend Jimmy Erdman.

The right thing to do would be to take the shoes off and tell Mr. Wheeler what he had done. But Wesley couldn't do that. He needed the new shoes. He didn't want to tell his mother what had happened to the first pair.

When Mr. Wheeler offered him a ride home, Wesley said he was going to walk. He wanted to break in the new shoes, he explained.

The real reason Wesley wanted to walk home had nothing to do with his new shoes. On the drive over to the shoe store, Wesley had noticed a sign in the window of a health food store—CREATINE ON SALE.

The bell over the door jingled gently when Wesley walked inside Nature's Garden. It was a small store, and quiet except for the sound of tinkly New Age music playing on the radio. A sign on the wall said . . .

IF I HAD KNOWN I WAS GOING
TO LIVE THIS LONG
I WOULD HAVE TAKEN
BETTER CARE OF MYSELF!

"May I help you?" asked the owner, a woman with wild black hair and lots of makeup who was sitting behind the cash register.

"No thank you," Wesley replied politely. "I'm just looking."

Wesley had never been in a health food store. He felt slightly embarrassed, as if he had wandered into the ladies' underwear section of a department store by accident. Looking around quickly, he hoped to spot a sign that would point him toward the creatine that was on sale. There was no such sign.

Nature's Garden wasn't like any other store Wesley had ever seen. As he walked down the aisle, he couldn't imagine what all those products were for, or who would buy them.

Pumpkin seed oil . . . vegetable soap . . . bee pollen capsules . . . bean pod tea . . . shark cartilage powder ("Sharks don't get cancer," the bottle claimed). Wesley remembered the old joke about carrots being good for your eyes because nobody ever saw a rabbit wearing glasses.

The front bell jingled and a little old lady came in. The owner went to take care of her. Wesley went off in search of creatine.

Toward the back of the store the brand names started to look more promising: Raw Energy . . . Body Ammo . . . Rocket Fuel Herbal Extract . . . Male Fuel . . . Turbo Charge . . . Power Pump Powder . . .

Then he spotted the creatine—nearly a whole aisle filled with jar after jar of it. Creatine powder and creatine pills. Chewable creatine. Creatine

Monohydrate. Mega Creatine. Creatine with Phosphatidylserine. Creatine Effervescent.

"Energize your muscles!" one of bottles shouted on the front. "Increase muscle size, power, and strength."

The bell on the door jingled again, but Wesley didn't notice. He had picked up a bottle from the shelf and was reading the label. . . .

"Creatine was developed by British physiologist Roger Harris and was first used by British sprinters in the 1992 Summer Olympics in Barcelona, Spain. It allows athletes to train at a higher intensity, which improves performance and helps you build muscle faster. . . ."

Wesley turned the bottle over, looking for a price tag.

Sale price: $29.99

Thirty bucks? For one bottle? Wesley looked more closely at the label and saw that the manufacturer recommended that users take creatine in two phases: a five-day "loading phase," in which you were supposed to take a bunch of doses in a short period of time, and then a "maintenance phase," in which you took it before every workout. The thirty-dollar bottle would last just five days, Wesley calculated.

Wesley pulled out his wallet. There was a five-dollar bill and some change inside. As he put the bottle of creatine back on the shelf, he noticed somebody at the other end of the aisle.

It was Jimmy Erdman.

There was no way to get out of the store without Jimmy's seeing him. Wesley looked around quickly, trying to find a product other than creatine he could have possibly come into the store to buy. There were some bags of potato chips on a rack nearby, so Wesley grabbed one and went over to Jimmy.

"Hey, man, what are you doing here?" he asked a little too cheerfully.

Jimmy looked up, alarmed. He hadn't expected to see anyone he knew shopping in Nature's Garden, much less his best friend.

"Just lookin' around," he said, putting a bottle on the shelf in front of him.

Wesley glanced at the bottle Jimmy had put back on the shelf.

"Super Fat Magnet," the label said in bold letters. "Advanced Electrostatic Formula Traps Fat."

"What's that stuff?" Wesley asked.

"What's it look like?" Jimmy said defensively.

"You're not so fat."

Even though he was trying to make Jimmy feel good, Wesley instantly regretted saying that. Jimmy was obviously fat. Everyone knew it. There was no point in trying to pretend he wasn't. But Wesley felt he had to say something, and those were the first words that popped into his mind. Jimmy looked at him, a sad frown on his face.

"Thanks for the compliment," he said. "I know I'm fat, Wes."

"What I mean is, I never thought it bothered you," Wesley said, trying to recover. "I mean, guys laugh at me for being skinny and I want to go hide. They laugh at you for being fat and you take a bow. Like it's a big joke. I wish I could handle it like you do."

"Wes," Jimmy said, "when they laugh at me, I want to hide, too. I can't. The way I hide it is to pretend it doesn't bother me."

"What do you need that stuff for anyway?" Wesley asked, pointing to the bottle of Super Fat Magnet. "Why don't you just stop eating?"

"It's not as simple as that," Jimmy informed his friend. "If you only knew what I've gone through trying to lose weight."

"May I help you boys?" the lady behind the cash register asked.

"We're just looking," they replied together.

Jimmy grabbed the bag of potato chips out of Wesley's hand. *Fat free! Salt free! Cholesterol free! Oven baked!* it said on the bag. "Something tells me you didn't come here to buy this cardboard," Jimmy said.

Sheepishly, Wesley led Jimmy down the aisle and pointed to the creatine.

"I came for this," Wesley admitted. Jimmy looked at the bottle. Then he looked at Wesley.

"What do you need that stuff for?" Jimmy asked, "Why don't you just start eating?"

Both boys laughed. Wesley and Jimmy had been best friends since first grade. They had talked about everything that two boys talk about. But not once in that time had either of them mentioned that the other was too fat or too skinny. Their weight problems had always been something they had only thought about, and now the subject was out in the open.

Despite the embarrassment of having his best friend find out his little secret, Wesley and Jimmy both left Nature's Garden (without buying anything) feeling better than they had when they walked in. Their secret was out, at least to each other.

Wesley and Jimmy always thought they were best friends because they enjoyed each other's company. They did. But there was more to it. For the first time, they had come to realize they had something else in common. And maybe that was the reason they had become such good friends in the first place.

10

Working Out

WESLEY BROWN WAS HAVING A DREAM. HE was in a professional wrestling match, and his opponent was Dr. Demented. It was a "steel cage match," in which a fifteen foot high cage is placed around the ring. The first man to climb out of the cage and touch the floor outside is the winner.

Dr. Demented was pummeling Wesley, of course. What could an eighty pound kid with no muscles do against one of the greatest wrestlers in the world? He picked Wesley up, spun him around, and tossed him across the ring like a Wiffle ball. He climbed up to the top of the ropes and jumped off, flattening Wesley like a piece of Silly Putty.

"Why did you tell your friend Jimmy I was Doctor Demented!" Dr. Demented shouted at Wesley. "You promised not to tell *anyone*!"

Then he picked Wesley up and mashed his head against the cage so hard, the wire sliced through his face like a cookie cutter through dough.

That was when Wesley woke up. He was shaking, terrified. But he was relieved, too. It was just a dream. Jimmy hadn't blabbed.

As Wesley was lying in bed trying to fall back asleep, he began thinking about everything. How skinny he was. How fat Jimmy was. How strong Mr. Wheeler was. That's when he came up with a brilliant idea—to ask Mr. Wheeler if he would help him and Jimmy build muscles.

It was perfect. Neither of the boys had enough money to buy the supplements they would need to build the body they wanted. Mr. Wheeler was built like a truck, and he had a gym in his garage. He was a great guy. Maybe he would show them what to do so they could have bodies like his. It was worth a shot anyway.

When Wesley brought the idea to Jimmy the next morning in homeroom, Jimmy didn't exactly jump up and down with excitement. He had tried exercising before, and he hated it. Jogging hurt his legs. He was no good at sports. And he didn't like the looks he got from other people when he worked out. He clung to the belief that there must be some pill he could take that would help him lose weight and build muscles.

During phys ed that day, Mr. Wheeler had the boys do what he called the "chin and hold." Each boy had to pull himself up to a chinning bar and see how long he could hold his chin above the bar. Mr. Wheeler stood below with a stopwatch to tell each boy his time.

Carl Campanella lasted a minute and forty seconds, the best in the class. Wesley lasted five seconds, and considered himself lucky to make it that long. Jimmy couldn't pull his weight up enough to get his chin over the bar.

When the laughter died down, Jimmy smiled at everybody and took his usual bows. But when he got to the end of the line, he pulled Wesley aside.

"I've had it," Jimmy said. "Let's try that idea of yours."

The two boys walked home from school that day rehearsing what they were going to say to Mr. Wheeler.

"Remember," Wesley warned Jimmy, "he doesn't know you know he's Doctor Demented. If he finds out you know, he'll probably kill both of us."

"I know. I know."

When they reached Briar Oak Avenue, they spotted Mr. Wheeler. He was already home from school, working in his garden.

"Don't look now," Jimmy whispered, "but I think Doctor Demented is trimming his petunias."

"Quiet, he'll hear you!"

Mr. Wheeler glanced up from his flowers, saw the boys coming toward him, and gave them a cheery hello.

"What can I do for you boys?"

"Uh, Mr. Wheeler," Wesley said, "we have a question."

"Fire away."

"How can we get muscles like yours?"

Mr. Wheeler wanted to laugh, but he could tell Wesley was serious, as well as a little embarrassed to ask the question. He took off his gardening gloves and put down his pruner.

"There's only one way to build muscle—weight training."

"Yeah, we want to do that," Wesley said.

"It's hard work. Are you boys prepared to work hard?"

"Yes."

"You have to be dedicated."

"We are."

"It will take a long time. I've been training with weights for fifteen years."

"Wow!"

"There are no shortcuts."

"Would you show us what to do?" Wesley asked.

"Did you get permission from your parents to do this?"

"Yes," the boys lied together.

"Okay, I'll design an exercise program for each

of you to get you started," Mr. Wheeler replied. "The rest is up to you."

"That's fair," Jimmy agreed.

"Good," Mr. Wheeler said, sticking out his massive hand for the boys to shake. "I work out early in the morning. You can use my equipment after school. How does that sound?"

"It's a deal."

"Good," Mr. Wheeler said. "Step into my office."

Mr. Wheeler opened his garage door, which faced the side of the house. Then he walked around the boys, looking them over.

It was not a pretty sight. Wesley slouched down and hunched his shoulders over in a lame attempt appear less skinny. Jimmy sucked in his gut so deeply that he was gasping for air. It was like a scene from an old Laurel and Hardy movie.

"The solution is simple," Mr. Wheeler finally announced. "All we need to do is slice thirty pounds off *you* and attach them to *you*."

Neither of the boys laughed even after Mr. Wheeler assured them that he was kidding, so he continued.

"Weight training will be beneficial to both of you. It will help you lose some of that extra weight you're carrying, Jimmy. For Wes, it will help you put some pounds on. And it will build muscle for both of you."

"Isn't it all genetics?" Jimmy asked. "I mean, my dad is fat. Maybe that's why I'm fat."

"Not all overweight guys have overweight kids," Mr. Wheeler pointed out. "And not all underweight guys have underweight kids."

"My mom says my dad was fat, too," Wesley pointed out.

"See what I mean?" said Mr. Wheeler. "It's not all genetics."

"Maybe it's all hormones," Jimmy suggested.

"Forget about those excuses," Mr. Wheeler said, raising his voice slightly. "You were born with a certain body type. You can make the most of that body by working out and eating right, or you can lay around feeling sorry for yourself and eating junk food. It's your choice."

Jimmy took a step backward. He had heard that tone of voice from grown-ups before, but never from a grown-up who once supposedly ripped a guy's ear off and ate it. Jimmy decided to stop whining and do whatever Mr. Wheeler told him to do.

First, Mr. Wheeler had the boys go through a series of stretching exercises, explaining that they could hurt themselves if they tried lifting too much weight without loosening up their muscles first.

Next, he had each boy lie back on an exercise bench and try to lift a barbell up from his chest and back down again. Landon Wheeler could bench press more than four hundred pounds. He put fifty pounds on Jimmy's bar and thirty-five pounds on Wesley's.

Wesley gripped the bar with both hands and pushed. The bar didn't move, so he pushed harder. That got the bar up a little, but Wesley had to push even harder to get it moving off the rack that held the weight over his head. He lowered the bar to his bony chest and rested it there for a moment. He was already panting and sweating.

Wesley glanced over at Jimmy. He was in the same position.

Straining, Wesley pushed the bar off his chest. Slowly, he raised it. His arms were quivering. His face was red.

"Push! Push! Push yourself!" Mr. Wheeler hollered at both boys. "If you want to build muscle, you're going to have to push your body to the limit. Don't hold back!"

Urged on by Mr. Wheeler, Wesley summoned up some unknown supply of energy and pushed the bar to its highest point. Then he let his arms collapse, allowing the weight to drop down to the rack over his head with a loud clank.

He was exhausted. He looked over to see Jimmy in the same condition.

"Good!" yelled Mr. Wheeler. "Next time, don't just *drop* the weight at the end. Gravity doesn't build muscles. Lower the bar *slowly*. Fight the weight coming down, just like you fought picking it up. You see, when you lift a weight, your muscle gets shorter. When you lower it, the muscle gets longer. It's when that muscle gets longer that you tear those muscle fibers."

"Why would we want to do that?" Jimmy asked, panting.

"Tearing muscle fiber is the whole point of weight training," Mr. Wheeler explained. "You want to slightly damage the muscle tissue. Then your body repairs the damage and builds a bigger, stronger muscle. Do that over and over again, and the muscle will get a little bigger and stronger each time you work out."

Mr. Wheeler had the boys do a few more exercises, then clapped his hands and told them their first session was finished.

"That's *it*?" Jimmy asked, rubbing his shoulder.

"My philosophy is, you work out hard and you work out fast. You don't work out long."

"Should we come back tomorrow?" Wesley asked.

"No. Come back the day after tomorrow. We only do weight training three days a week."

"Wouldn't we build muscles faster if we lifted weights every day?" Jimmy asked.

"That's what everybody thinks," Mr. Wheeler replied. "But your muscles don't grow while you're working out. They grow when you're *resting*. They need time to recover from the damage you just did to them. If you start working out before a muscle is rebuilt, it throws off the whole process."

Wesley was fascinated, thinking about how the insides of his body worked. It reminded him of the days he used to examine insects under his microscope.

"I'll design an exercise program for each of you," Mr. Wheeler told the boys as he escorted them out of the garage. "I'll tell you what muscle groups you're going to work on each day, how many reps you're going to do, how many sets, and how much weight you're going to lift. I don't want either of you to pick up a pound more than you can handle safely. Okay?"

"Okay!"

"Good. You boys run along now. If I don't replant these tulips I'm going to be in big trouble."

On the way home, Wesley rubbed his arms. He could already feel some soreness, which he took as a sign that he had damaged his muscles correctly.

"You know what's the first thing we should do once we have muscles?" Jimmy asked.

"What?"

"Kick Carl Campanella's butt."

11

The Importance of Muscles

WHEN WESLEY BROWN WOKE UP THE NEXT morning, he couldn't move. His arms felt like they were made of concrete. His legs felt like they had been run over by a steamroller. His whole body was sore, with the exception of his eyelids, which opened and closed again right away.

At first Wesley thought he might have died, and this was what it felt like to be dead. But if he was dead, he thought, why did he feel pain? Dead people shouldn't feel pain. And why did his clock radio just click on? Dead people can't listen to the radio. Or can they?

"Get up, y'all!" the Q102 morning DJ Mark Harris shouted with much too much enthusiasm. "It's seven o'clock and it's a beautiful Q102 day. We're gonna find out what's goin' on out on the roads from our traffic reporter Darla Morris."

"Mark, we got a major tie-up coming into

Houston. A jackknifed tractor trailer dumped a thousand rolls of toilet paper on Route 45. So nothing is moving out here."

"Let's just hope nobody's bowels start movin', eh, Darla?"

"Ha-ha. That's funny, Mark."

"Hey, Darla, what *is* a bowel, anyway, and where do they move to?"

"I just report the traffic, Mark."

"Too bad. If anybody knows what a bowel is, call or fax our special request hotline, will ya? Inquiring minds want to know."

Wesley groaned. He somehow summoned the strength to lift himself out of bed and pull some clothes out of his closet.

As he struggled to put his pants on, he consoled himself with the thought that he must have ripped a whole lot of those muscle fibers working out with Mr. Wheeler the previous day. He ripped 'em good, because it hurt so much. He hoped that while he was sleeping, those muscles were busy rebuilding themselves into bigger and stronger muscles. Looking in the mirror as he brushed his teeth, he didn't think his arms appeared to be any larger.

"Here's the news, y'all!" Mark Harris babbled on the radio. "There was a big train wreck in Japan last night that killed a few hundred people. But who cares about that, anyway? The big news is that professional wrestling is coming to the Humble Civic Center in little old Humble, Texas on October 19th!"

Wesley forgot about his aches and pains for a moment and ran to the radio to turn up the volume.

"Houston gets rasslin' all the time, but you hicks in the 'burbs ain't never seen the likes of an AWF SkullCrush show! You gonna get to see Jerry Spitfire fighting The Annihilator. You gonna see Deadman against The Nuclear Menace. And the main event is gonna be Subhuman Newman versus the one and only Doctor Demented! Right in your own backyard. It's gonna be The Rumble in Humble! Darla, you still there?"

"Yes, Mark," she replied wearily.

"They say the Doctor Demented guy once bit off somebody's ear and ate it, Darla."

"That's disgusting!"

"Well, maybe he cooked it first, Darla."

"I have to go, Mark."

"You have to go? Better grab one of those toilet paper rolls off the road first, Darla! Ha-ha-ha! And let us know if everything comes out okay. Get it? Ha-ha-ha-ha!"

Wesley grabbed a pencil and jotted down the vital information about the wrestling match. He ran downstairs excitedly.

"Mom!" he shouted, "they're going to have wrestling at the Civic Center! Can I go?"

Bonnie Brown was in the kitchen sipping a cup

of coffee. Wesley's breakfast was on the table waiting for him.

She sighed. She expected there to be wrestling at the Astrodome in Houston. But in Humble? They had removed the seesaws from the playground at Wesley's old elementary school because parents were afraid kids were going to get hurt on them. But then they were bringing in pro wrestling? It didn't make sense. Kids needed seesaws. They didn't need professional wrestling.

She sighed again. She had a tough enough time monitoring the violence Wesley was exposed to on TV and CDs without having to worry about *this*.

"Can I go, Mom?" Wesley asked, grabbing the box of Raisin Bran.

"We'll talk about it."

"What does that mean?"

"It means we'll talk about it."

"Why can't we talk about it right now?"

"I have to think about it first."

"That means no," Wesley whined. "Every time you have to think about something before we can talk about it, it means the answer is going to be no."

"It doesn't mean no. It just means I have to think about it."

Wesley went to school angry.

Over the next few weeks Wesley and Jimmy went to Mr. Wheeler's garage every other day after school. When their workout day fell on a Saturday, they showed up without fail. Mr. Wheeler had custom-designed a weight-training program for each boy, depending on his body type. He led them through each session, spotting them, making sure they did each exercise correctly, encouraging them, and yelling at them occasionally to get the best out of them.

Wesley and his mother had been arguing about the upcoming Rumble in Humble at the Civic Center. First she said she didn't want Wesley to go, then she changed her mind. Then she told him she was having second thoughts. In the meantime, she had also been expressing disapproval over Wesley's weight training at Mr. Wheeler's house.

It wasn't that Bonnie Brown had anything against muscles. She just wasn't happy with what a boy like Wesley had to go through to get them.

In Bonnie's mind, anybody who spent a lot of time or money trying to make himself *look good* had problems. To her, men who pumped iron were just like women who fussed with their hair and makeup for hours on end. They seemed dumb, shallow, their priorities backward. Life was too short to waste it looking in a mirror, according to Bonnie Brown.

Of course, Bonnie had been beautiful without trying since she was a little girl. She didn't have to spend time trying to make herself look good. She woke up in the morning and she looked great, even in her thirties.

When Wesley would come home from Mr. Wheeler's house talking about his reps and sets and curls and squats, Bonnie became more and more concerned about her son. He seemed like he was becoming obsessed. He seemed like he was turning into his father.

"Why is this so important?" she finally asked him one day two weeks after he started working out. "It's not healthy."

"Mr. Wheeler says weight training is the healthiest thing you can do for your body," Wesley replied.

"I mean it's not healthy for your *mind*. Why don't you try to build up your mind instead of just making muscles?"

"Mom, when I walk into school, the other kids don't see my mind. They see my body. They judge me by what I look like. And I look terrible."

"You look *fine*," his mother responded. "You want the kind of friends who like people because they have muscles? What kind of friends are *they* going to be?"

"I just want to feel good about myself. Mr. Wheeler says he used to be skinny like me. After he built himself up, he was more confident and people liked him more."

"Maybe I should have a talk with this Mr. Wheeler."

"Are you saying I can't work out with him anymore?"

"I didn't say that. I simply said I should talk to him about this. Having big muscles just isn't important, Wesley!"

"It's important to *me*."

12

A Twinkle in His Eyes

LANDON WHEELER WAS COOKING A TOFU broccoli stir-fry when the doorbell rang. He had to be very careful to turn down the stove so his brown rice wouldn't burn. He wiped his hands on his apron so he could turn the doorknob.

"Mr. Wheeler, my name is Bonnie Brown. Wesley's mom. Can I talk with you for a few minutes?"

"Of course!" Mr. Wheeler wiped his hands hastily on his apron again before shaking hands. "Please come in. Wesley is a wonderful boy. Can I offer you a cup of coffee, Bonnie? Decaf?"

"No thank you. What smells so good?"

"It's tofu stir-fry with broccoli over brown rice. Would you like some?"

"No thank you."

Bonnie sat on the couch and glanced around the living room quickly. Wesley had told her that Mr.

Wheeler wasn't married. She had figured a single, bodybuilding gym teacher's house would be decorated with wall-to-wall mirrors, or maybe a pommel horse in the middle of the living room. The antique pine furniture and African masks took her by surprise. So did the music she thought she recognized, playing softly on the stereo.

"Is that Brahms?" she asked.

"Actually it's Beethoven's violin concerto, in D major."

Bonnie felt like she had just stepped into a parallel universe. A man who cooked, enjoyed classical music, and collected African art? And yet he was a gym teacher who had muscles out to *here*. This guy had to be some kind of mutant! And why did he have a copy of *Gray's Anatomy* on his coffee table?

"Is anything the matter with Wesley?" Mr. Wheeler asked after they had made some small talk.

"No," Bonnie replied. "Well, yes, in a way. I'm concerned about him. All this weightlifting . . . I mean, clearly he feels insecure about being skinny and he's trying to fit in with the other boys at school by trying to make himself muscular. But he seems almost obsessed with it."

"I understand your concern," Mr. Wheeler replied. "Let me ask you something. Does Wesley do any other exercise? Does he play a sport outside of school?"

"No. Not really."

"As a phys ed instructor, I think *that's* something parents should be concerned about. Kids today spend most of their time staring into screens. TV screens. Computer screens. Movie screens. Being slim doesn't mean a boy or girl is in shape. Even boys like Wesley need some kind of exercise. A well-monitored program of weight training isn't going to hurt him. In my view, it's going to make Wesley healthier, and improve his self-esteem. If he gets a few muscles along the way, what's so terrible about that?"

"But what about this fixation he has with professional wrestling?" Bonnie Brown asked. "It seems to me that the wrestling and the weightlifting may be connected. I don't want my son turning into a violent person."

Landon Wheeler shifted uncomfortably in his chair. He had spent a lot of time thinking about that problem. *What if wrestling* is *a bad influence on children?* he often asked himself. *What if some kid saw Doctor Demented hit a man in the ring, then went home and smacked his little brother? Would it be my fault?*

Mr. Wheeler always felt a little uncomfortable when the subject of professional wrestling came up. Just talking about it might give away his secret, he feared. He had taken the precaution of storing his Dr. Demented costume in a locked closet after Wesley's dog sniffed it out.

"I've read a lot of scientific studies," Mr. Wheeler explained. "Some experts say watching violence makes young people act violently. Others believe watching violence helps them blow off steam and actually *prevents* them from acting out their own violent tendencies. But I'll tell you this from my experience. Many of the boys in my classes at school are wrestling fans, Bonnie. They know it's staged. They like the theater of it, the drama. Professional wrestling is like a soap opera for boys."

Bonnie Brown was staring intently at Mr. Wheeler, but she wasn't completely concentrating on what he was saying. She was staring at his eyes. They were the bluest, most intense eyes she'd ever seen.

"Personally," Mr. Wheeler continued, "I think watching wrestling is harmless. Kids are better at distinguishing between reality and fantasy than we think they are. I have never seen one of my students act out what he saw in a wrestling match. If I ever did, I would have to rethink my opinion."

Bonnie Brown noticed that Mr. Wheeler had finished talking, so she forced herself to stop looking at his eyes. She wasn't sure that she agreed with what he'd said, but his explanation sounded good anyway.

"I respect your opinion as an educator, Mr. Wheeler," she said, rising to her feet. "And I thank you for taking the time to speak with me."

"Please, call me Landon."

Mr. Wheeler rushed to open the door for her, at the same time fumbling for something in his pocket.

"I have a couple of good seats to the Rumble in Humble next week," he said, pulling out two tickets. "Doctor Demented versus somebody called Subhuman Newman. You and Wesley can have them if you'd like."

"Where did you get these?"

"From a guy I know," he lied. In fact, the AWF slipped him a few ringside passes every time he wrestled.

Bonnie Brown looked at the tickets. The price on each one was one hundred dollars. She hated everything to do with wrestling. But Wesley's birthday was coming up. She hadn't bought him a present yet. He *had* done well on his last report card. And the tickets, after all, were free.

She took the tickets. "Do you have another one?" she asked. "Maybe you can join us."

Mr. Wheeler looked at Bonnie Brown for a moment. Was she asking him out on a *date*? He wasn't sure. Maybe she was just being friendly by inviting him along. In any case, he couldn't go because he would be in the ring that evening beating up Subhuman Newman. But he was intrigued. He had forgotten all about his tofu stir-fry.

"Uh, I'm going to be busy that night," he replied

cautiously. "But maybe we could get together for dinner sometime."

Bonnie Brown looked at Landon Wheeler. Did he just ask her out on a *date*? She wasn't sure. Maybe he was just being friendly.

"You mean Wesley and you and I could get together for dinner?" she asked. If he was going to ask her for a date, she decided, she was going to make him come out and say it.

"Actually I was thinking just you and me."

Bonnie Brown blushed. She couldn't remember the last time a man had asked her out. She didn't meet many single men. She didn't quite know how to respond. Maybe he was just joking. She had to be sure.

"You mean we should go out to dinner to discuss Wesley's situation at school?" she asked.

"We don't necessarily have to talk about Wesley," Mr. Wheeler replied with a twinkle in his eyes.

That's good enough for me, Bonnie Brown said to herself. He had just asked her out on an honest-to-goodness date. Bonnie felt her heart beating as she fumbled for the doorknob. She hadn't felt this way since high school.

"I'd love to," she found herself responding.

Wesley sat home chewing his nails, waiting for his mother to get back from Mr. Wheeler's house. *What could be taking her so long?* he wondered.

She was probably giving him her usual speech about how bodybuilding was for muscleheads without brains. He guessed that she was telling Mr. Wheeler to leave her son alone and stop weight training him.

Wesley peeked through the curtain and saw his mother coming up the front steps. He raced to the couch and jumped on it, just in time to look like he had been watching TV when the door opened.

Bonnie Brown came in the room with a dazed look on her face. She looked like she had been sleepwalking. She didn't say anything to Wesley.

"Are you okay, Mom?"

"Sure, I'm okay," she replied. "What makes you think I'm not okay?"

"Your face is a little flushed or something."

"I'm fine."

Wesley waited for his mother to let him know the result of her meeting with Mr. Wheeler, but she just stood there.

"So, can I keep working out with Mr. Wheeler?" Wesley asked.

"Sure. I guess so," she replied absently.

Wesley looked at his mother in disbelief. He'd never seen her like this. She was just standing there, like she had walked into a room and didn't remember why she was there.

"Well, what did Mr. Wheeler say?" Wesley asked.

"He . . . invited me out for dinner," she replied with a little giggle.

"He asked you to go out on a *date*?" Wesley asked, stupefied.

"What's wrong with that? He seems nice. He's about my age. He's single, very handsome."

"You're going out with—" Wesley was about to say "Doctor Demented" but he caught himself. "You're going out with my *gym teacher*?"

"Sure, why not? Oh, he gave me these . . ."

She pulled the tickets out of her pocket and handed them to Wesley.

"Two ringside tickets to The Rumble in Humble? Sweet! I thought you *hated* wrestling. These are hundred dollar seats, Mom!"

"Think of it as your birthday present."

"He gave you these? Did he . . . tell you much about himself?"

"A little," she replied. "He's into cooking and decorating. He loves classical music and he wants to be a doctor."

He already is a doctor, Wesley thought to himself. *He's Doctor Demented. And soon he might be my mother's boyfriend.*

13

Carl Campanella

"NICE SHOES, MOUSE."

Every time Carl Campanella walked past Wesley Brown, that's what he would say. If nobody was around, he would say it out loud with a smirk and a sneer. If he walked by Wesley when there was a teacher nearby, Carl would whisper it.

"Nice shoes, Mouse. Where'dja get 'em?"

Carl Campanella hated the fact that although he'd hung Wesley Brown's shoes on a wire outside school, Wesley showed up at school the very next day wearing the exact same shoes.

When Carl Campanella decided to torment a kid, he expected that kid to *stay* tormented. He wanted that kid to be defeated, humiliated, traumatized, maybe even psychologically scarred for life. What was the fun of bothering someone if it didn't even seem to bother him?

When Carl saw Wesley walking around wearing

the same shoes he had so carefully slung around the telephone wire, he took it as a personal insult. He was determined to make Wesley pay.

Wesley Brown was equally determined not to let anything happen to his second pair of shoes. He dug out the old combination lock he used to put on his bike, and brought it to phys ed with him every day. Instead of casually tossing his clothes into an empty locker before gym class, he shut the door and locked it.

It was after phys ed one day when Carl Campanella made his move. The boys' locker room was jammed with bodies as everyone hurried to get dressed.

Wesley pulled off his T-shirt and put on his long-sleeved shirt as quickly as possible in hopes that the other boys wouldn't see his skinny chest.

Carl Campanella had no problem taking his shirt off in front of other people. He had big biceps, and he liked to show them off. Carl usually strutted around after phys ed in his underwear, snapping a towel at the other boys or telling dirty jokes.

Wesley noticed Carl looking at him as he bent down to tie his shoes. When Carl started coming over to him, Wesley expected Carl to threaten him or something. But he didn't.

"Excuse me, Mouse," Carl said politely as he held his math book open. "I just don't get this stuff about isosceles triangles. Can you help me?"

Wesley looked up at Carl. He had this very pleading, serious look on his face. Wesley didn't entirely trust Carl. It looked like a trick. But there was that small chance that Carl was being sincere. Maybe if he helped Carl with his geometry, Wesley figured, Carl might pay him back by leaving him alone.

"An isosceles triangle has two sides that are the same length," Wesley explained, "and it has two equal angles."

"But what about scalene triangles?" Carl asked. "Aren't they the same?" A few of Carl's friends had gathered around to watch the lesson, Wesley noticed from the corner of his eye.

"No," he continued. "In a scalene triangle, the sides and angles are unequal."

Wesley thought he heard a few of the boys snickering. Most kids his age, he knew, thought geometry was for dorks. And a lot of them thought trying to get good grades in *any* subject was for dorks.

"A scalene triangle looks kind of tilted," Wesley went on, as Carl looked on attentively. He really seemed like he was trying to understand.

It was while Wesley was explaining scalene triangles that he thought he smelled something. He wasn't sure what it was, and he didn't think anything of it at first.

"A right triangle can have different sides and angles, but one of the angles has to be ninety degrees—"

Wesley looked up. A bunch of boys were standing around looking at him, trying to suppress laughter. Jimmy Erdman was at the edge of the group, Wesley noticed. Jimmy was looking at Wesley's feet. Wesley looked down.

His shoelaces were on fire.

The whole time Wesley had been patiently explaining triangles to Carl Campanella, one of Carl's friends had been on his hands and knees holding a cigarette lighter to his laces. The flames were licking the bottom of Wesley's pants.

Wesley jumped, and the locker room erupted into laughter. When Wesley slapped at the flames to put them out, Carl Campanella and his friends hooted with glee.

"Mouse, your feet stink," one of the boys said.

"Let's get out of here before the smoke detector goes off," said another.

"Yeah, it's too hot in here," Carl Campanella said, turning to leave. "Thanks for the help, Mouse. You're a real math genius."

Carl and his friends strutted out of the locker room, cackling and smacking each other on the back like they had just won the Super Bowl. Soon all the boys had left, leaving Jimmy and Wesley alone.

"You okay?" Jimmy asked as Wesley examined his charred laces.

Wesley looked at him.

"You want to know if I'm okay *now*?" he asked

bitterly. "Where were you when Campanella was torching my shoes?"

"What could I do about it?"

"*Something!*" Wesley shouted. "You could have at least *said* something. You could have let me know what he was doing."

"He would have kicked my butt," Jimmy replied lamely.

"Friends help friends," Wesley muttered. He pulled the burned lace out of one shoe and used what was left of it to hold the shoe together until he could get home and replace the laces. "Thanks for nothing."

"I'm sorry, man," Jimmy said. "I was afraid."

14

Good Heat

LANDON WHEELER PREPARED FOR A DATE
with a woman almost exactly the same way he
prepared for one of his wrestling matches. He ran
a mile, did a hundred sit-ups and a hundred push-
ups, and took a shower. Then he would sit and
read *Better Homes and Gardens* while sipping
from a bottle of carrot juice until it was time for
him to make his entrance.

Dating was harder than fighting, though. Beating
guys up, Mr. Wheeler had noticed, was a lot easier
than talking to a woman he didn't know very well.

The biggest difference between a date and a fight
was that for a date, he didn't put on his Dr. Demented mask and costume. He put on a newly
pressed pair of tan pants, his best shirt, and a clean
sport jacket. He wanted to impress his date, the
same way he wanted to impress wrestling fans
with his performance in the ring.

A good wrestling match always starts with a "pop"—a loud reaction from the crowd to something the wrestler does. You might get a pop by coming into the ring wearing a cool costume, or you might get a pop by attacking your opponent with a baseball bat before the fight even begins. Anything to get the crowd into the action right away.

When Landon Wheeler showed up at Bonnie Brown's door, he hid a bouquet of red roses behind his back. That, he figured, would start the date off with a good pop.

He didn't date a lot. Women found him attractive, he knew that. But once they got to know him, they would start asking him questions he didn't like to answer: *How did you get that bruise on your face? Why are you "busy" most Friday and Saturday nights? What mysterious thing are you up to? Why can't I come with you?. Why don't you like to talk about yourself?*

Because he kept his wrestling career a secret, women found Landon Wheeler to be a little creepy.

Bonnie Brown didn't date much either. She found most men she met to be either married or stupid, and frequently both. Besides, who had the time? After she came home from work and made dinner for Wesley, she had little energy to go out on dates.

It had been a long time since Bonnie had been

out alone with another adult. She still hadn't gotten used to the idea that Wesley was old enough to stay home without a baby-sitter.

"There's frozen pizza in the fridge," she instructed Wesley as she rushed to put on her earrings before Mr. Wheeler showed up. "If there's an emergency, the phone number of the restaurant is on the pad in the kitchen."

"I'll be *fine*," Wesley assured her. "You go have a good time, Mom."

The doorbell rang. When Landon handed Bonnie the flowers, he got just the pop he had been hoping for. Bonnie's mouth dropped open in surprise. No man had *ever* given her flowers. Not even her ex-husband.

After that first pop, a wrestler wants to generate as much "heat" as possible during the match. Roughly translated, "heat" means "excitement." He wants the crowd to watch him, to wonder what incredible move he's going to pull next. He wants them to be fascinated by him, to get emotional about him. There can be good heat or bad heat. But if there's no heat at all, that's when the crowd starts chanting, *"Borrrrrrrrrrrrrrrrrrrringgggggg!"*

Landon took Bonnie's hand and escorted her down the steps like she was the Queen of England. He told her how lovely she looked. He opened the car door for her. It was good heat.

When they got to the restaurant, Landon slipped the waiter a five dollar bill and they were led to a quiet table in the corner. He pulled out Bonnie's chair for her to sit down. He ordered a bottle of wine—in French. He expertly swirled the wine around in the glass and tasted it to make sure it was perfect. His table manners were impeccable.

Bonnie Brown was impressed. The last man who asked her out took her to a hockey game and spilled beer on her skirt. She felt instantly comfortable with Landon Wheeler.

She was amazed that he was well-versed in any subject she brought up. He knew about opera, classical music, and modern dance. He had seen a lot of movies, and not just the ones with chase scenes and explosions. They had read many of the same books. She was fascinated by his interest in collecting African masks.

Things were going great, Mr. Wheeler thought to himself as the food arrived. He hadn't generated such good heat since the time he fought Chainsaw Greg Horwitz for the AWF belt a few years back. As they chatted, he started thinking about a big finish—the pin. The knockout. The stunt that would have the crowd (that is, Bonnie Brown) cheering and wanting to come back for more.

By the time they were halfway done eating, they had finished the bottle of wine and Bonnie was feeling a little lightheaded. Eventually the conversation shifted to Wesley, and Bonnie's concern about his interest in professional wrestling.

"Don't you think it's stupid?" she asked with a

little giggle. "All those sweaty slobs in goofy costumes pretending to throw each other around? It's not just violent, it's so childish!"

"Uh, yeah," Landon Wheeler replied. "Childish."

"If you ask me," Bonnie continued, her tongue loosened by the wine, "the popularity of wrestling shows how pathetic so many men are these days. I mean, the average guy's biggest challenge in life is finding a parking spot each morning. Watching professional wrestling must be the only way they can fantasize about the good old days when men were men. Don't you think?"

"Interesting theory . . ."

Landon Wheeler had begun sweating the moment the topic of wrestling came up. It was one subject he didn't want to discuss. When they had been talking about music, movies, and literature, he was in control. He had been carefully guiding the rhythm of the date, the same way he guided the rhythm of his fights. But now, he had lost the heat. He remembered a match he'd had with The Memphis Mauler where the exact same thing happened. He had to do something, and fast.

"I really don't like the idea of this wrestling garbage being put on live in Humble," Bonnie continued. "How do you feel about it?"

"Would you excuse me for a moment?"

In wrestling, they call it a "resthold." This is when a guy has been jumping all over the ring and needs a break to catch his breath and plan his next series of moves. He'll put the other guy in a head-lock. Or he'll lay on the canvas with the other guy sitting on him for a minute or so. Anything to get his heart rate back to normal and figure out how he can turn the heat back on.

Landon scurried off to the men's room for a resthold. He washed his hands a few times and combed his hair. He desperately tried to think of a way to move the conversation away from wrestling. And he needed to come up with a big finish that would make Bonnie want to go out with him again.

"Did you notice that Cubist poster on the wall?" he asked Bonnie when he returned to the table. "Is that a Picasso or a Braque?"

"Their styles were so similar," Bonnie replied. "Did you ever see Picasso's *Accordionist*? It's virtually identical to Braque's *The Portuguese*."

Landon breathed a silent sigh of relief as soon as Bonnie began talking about modern art. If he could keep the conversation away from wrestling, he would be in good shape. He didn't want to attack wrestling, and he didn't want to defend it either. More than anything, he didn't want to let her know that he was a professional wrestler. Not on their first date, anyway.

Landon paid the check and helped Bonnie on with her coat. As they were waiting outside the restaurant for the valet to bring his car, he still hadn't come up with a big finish.

Several people were waiting in a line for their cars. That's when a man who looked to be homeless approached the line.

"Spare change, anyone?" he asked. "I want to buy something to eat."

"Why don't you get a *job*?" one of the men in line said to the homeless man. "I'm not going to give you money just so you can buy yourself a bottle of booze."

The homeless man stopped and put his face close to the man who made the remark.

"Did you have a drink with your dinner this evening, sir?"

"Don't talk to me like that, you bum!" the man said, pushing the homeless guy away.

"I'll talk any way I want!" the homeless guy said, pushing right back.

The people in line looked around nervously. It appeared as if there was about to be a fight. Landon Wheeler jumped between the two men and separated them with his powerful arms.

"Gentlemen," he said, smiling, "life is too short to bicker over such little things." Landon pushed the bill he was going to give to the parking attendant into the homeless man's hand.

"Get yourself something to eat, friend. And have a good night."

The homeless guy took the bill and walked away gratefully. The other guy seemed relieved that no punches had been thrown.

"I dig your car, man," the parking attendant said to Landon Wheeler as he handed over the keys.

Bonnie Brown looked at Landon like he was Abraham Lincoln, Gandhi, and Martin Luther King Jr. all rolled into one. Any man who could defuse a potentially violent confrontation so peacefully was a saint in her book.

Landon Wheeler knew he had the big finish he had been looking for. The match was over. Dr. Demented was victorious once again.

Back home, Wesley popped some microwave popcorn and flipped through the channels on the TV. He couldn't pay much attention, though. He was thinking about what his mother was doing.

Wesley had mixed feelings about her going out on a date with Mr. Wheeler. He was a great guy and all. But after all, he was a *guy*. A guy was a potential husband. A potential husband was a potential stepfather. Even though Wesley always wondered what it would be like to have a father, he wasn't sure he liked the idea of having a father after all the years of him and his mom being a team of two.

Wesley went to bed around eleven o'clock, but he was still awake when the door opened downstairs an hour later. His mom came up the stairs to check on him.

"So . . . how did it go?" Wesley asked. "Did he show you his barbell collection?"

"No." She laughed. "It went well, actually. We went to a French restaurant. He was the perfect gentleman. He even pulled my chair out for me."

In his mind, Wesley imagined Dr. Demented pulling his mother's chair out for her and then slamming some guy over the head with it. But there was a look on her face that he'd never seen before. She had a little secret smile. There was a sparkle in her eyes, a glow.

"Are you in love with Mr. Wheeler?" Wesley asked.

Bonnie Brown giggled. "Don't be silly!" she said. "I just met the man!"

She's in love, Wesley thought to himself. *My mother is in love with Doctor Demented. Doctor Demented is going to be my new father. I'll have to change my name to Wesley Demented.*

"If he asked you to marry him, would you?"

"Of course not!" she insisted. "That's crazy! I hardly know him."

She would, Wesley thought to himself.

"I bet you like those arms he's got, huh?"

"Arms?" Bonnie Brown laughed. "That's ridiculous! Do you think I would go out with a man because he's got big arms?"

Yes, Wesley thought to himself. *All girls like guys with big muscles. I'm going to have a new dad.*

"What did you talk about?" he asked.

"You know, grown-up things. Art, cooking, music. He's very well read."

"Did you talk about wrestling at all?" Wesley asked as casually as possible.

"A little. He didn't have much to say, come to think of it."

"Would you go out with him again?"

"If he asks me."

15

PAWS

"HUGS NOT THUGS! HUGS NOT THUGS!"

Wesley had flipped on the TV when he came home from school. He was chugging his usual Weight-On shake when the local news came on. He almost spit the shake when he saw his mother on the screen.

"Stop the violence!" she was chanting with a group of women who were parading around the Humble Civic Center holding picket signs—WRESTLING MUST GO! NOT IN OUR TOWN! MORONS GO HOME!

Wesley turned up the volume.

"It's the Grumble in Humble," the reporter said, "They call themselves PAWS—Parents Against Wrestling Stupidity. These moms are up in arms because quiet little Humble is about to be attacked by body slams, pile drivers, choker holds, and mayhem like this sleepy town has never seen before. Professional wrestling is coming to the Humble Civic Center next week and these women don't like it one bit. Excuse me, ma'am, what's your gripe with pro wrestling?"

"Professional wrestling is a bad influence on children," the woman replied. "If my kids want to see clowns, I'll take them to the circus."

The picket line kept moving and the reporter stuck the microphone into Bonnie Brown's face. Wesley put down his shake.

"Isn't wrestling just harmless fun?" the reporter asked.

"I don't believe it is," Wesley's mother replied. "Many studies have shown that children who are exposed to violence become more violent themselves. My son loves professional wrestling, but I don't want him emulating these muscle-bound buffoons."

"Will you let your son attend this show?"

"Well, I must admit it. His birthday is coming up. Somebody gave me free tickets, and I decided to let him go."

"A wrestler who calls himself Doctor Demented will be headlining the show," the reporter said. "If you could send a message to Doctor Demented, what would it be?"

"As far as I'm concerned," Bonnie Brown replied, "Doctor Demented can drop dead."

"There you have it. Reporting live—"

Wesley flipped off the TV and shook his head. At

some point his mother would have to find out that Mr. Wheeler—the guy she went on a date with on Friday night—was really Dr. Demented. Wesley just hoped he could be there to see her face when she found out.

Wesley went to his room, took off his school clothes, and put on his sweats. Then he hurried over to Mr. Wheeler's house for his workout.

"Where's Jimmy?" Mr. Wheeler asked when Wesley yanked open the garage door.

"I don't think he's coming," Wesley replied. "We had a little argument yesterday."

"Anything serious?"

"Not really. Hey, did you see the news a few minutes ago?"

"No, I was in here getting some extra work in to prepare for Saturday night," Mr. Wheeler replied. "What's up?"

"A bunch of women are protesting over at the Civic Center. They're trying to stop The Rumble in Humble."

"Is that so?"

"That's not all," Wesley continued. "One of them is my mom. They even interviewed her on TV. She said wrestlers are just muscle-bound buffoons, and she said she wished Doctor Demented would drop dead."

Landon Wheeler sighed. Every time he found a woman he really liked, something went wrong. It was only a matter of time before the woman would find out he was Dr. Demented, and then she would dump him. That was why he moved to Humble in the first place. A woman he had been dating in Oklahoma City was horrified when she found out what he did, and she got people around there so worked up over it that he had to move away.

He was in a bind. If he gave up the Dr. Demented character or quit wrestling entirely, he couldn't earn enough money to go to medical school. And they didn't hand out scholarships to thirty-five-year-old gym teachers who wanted to quit their jobs and become doctors.

"When are you going to tell her the truth?" Wesley asked.

"I don't know."

"You've got to tell her sometime."

"I know. But she'll hate me. She's so anti-wrestling, antiviolent."

"Yeah," Wesley agreed. "Once we had some cockroaches in our house, and my mom wouldn't even kill them. She captured them in a jar and released them outside."

"I don't know what to do," Mr. Wheeler admitted.

"Do you want *me* to tell her you're Doctor Demented?"

"No!"

Wesley went through the workout Mr. Wheeler

had designed for him, doing a series of front squats, one-legged calf raises, leg extensions, and barbell shrugs. Each exercise had a very specific number of sets and reps, and Mr. Wheeler told Wesley exactly how much weight he was supposed to lift. After thirty minutes of this, Wesley was exhausted.

Wesley had been working out at Mr. Wheeler's house every other day for four weeks. Each night he would look at himself in the mirror, examining himself for any sign of muscle growth. A little bulk. Some definition. *Anything*. So far, nothing. He looked like the same old scrawny weakling he always was.

"I'll never have arms like you," Wesley complained.

"Maybe not," Mr. Wheeler said. "But you'll get stronger. Just give it time. Rome wasn't built in a day. Neither were these pecs."

16

The Best Birthday
Present

THE HUMBLE CIVIC CENTER WAS TINY COM-
pared to the Astrodome. It only seated a few
thousand people. But that made it more intimate,
if that word could be used to describe a professional wrestling match. Unlike the Astrodome,
every seat in the Civic Center was close to the
action.

Fans surged through the turnstiles excitedly,
mostly teenage boys and their fathers. Many of
them had never seen wrestling in person.

PAWS (Parents Against Wrestling Stupidity) had
failed to keep wrestling out of Humble, but the
group decided to continue its protest anyway in
the hope of drawing attention to the violence
going on inside. A line of fifteen women marched
back and forth in front of the entrance to the Civic
Center, chanting and holding up signs.

Bonnie Brown pulled her car into the parking

lot, with Wesley at her side. She had thought about using her ticket, but decided her place was on the picket line.

"Why don't you come in and see the show, Mom?" Wesley asked.

"I don't want to see what goes on in there," she replied, taking her STOP THE VIOLENCE sign out of the trunk.

"But how can you protest against something you've never seen before?"

"I know what goes on," his mother said, handing Wesley his ticket. "You have a good time. I'll meet you out here when it's over."

She ran her fingers through his hair and wished him a happy birthday.

"Ladies and gentlemen," the ring announcer boomed into the microphone. "Welcome to the Humble Civic Center. We are so happy to bring you the finest quality AWF entertainment right here in the beautiful town of Humble, Texas!"

The crowd let out a cheer that the protestors outside on the street could hear.

"Fans, you will find programs, souvenirs, and delicious snacks in the concession area near the advance ticket window. But you won't want to miss any of the action, which begins right now with our opening match of the evening, a cruiser-weight battle!"

A buzz went through the crowd as a big, dark-haired man made his way into the ring. He was wearing a white bathrobe with the word SPITFIRE embroidered on the back.

"In this corner, from Tomball, Texas, is . . . Jerry Spitfire, the Texas Terror!"

Spitfire climbed into the ring, peeled off the robe, and flexed his muscles for the crowd. He was big, but not enormous like a heavyweight. Spitfire had not yet appeared on national TV, so most people in the crowd had never heard of him. But they cheered anyway, simply because he was there and they were seeing it live.

The smoke machines were smaller at the Humble Civic Center, the strobe lights and fireworks less spectacular. Professional wrestling in Humble was obviously a lower budget operation. The wrestlers would have to generate the excitement without the aid of special effects.

"And in this corner, from the African nation of Uganda, wrestling in America for the first time, is . . . The Annihilator!"

The Annihilator was actually an African-American auto mechanic from Indiana named Ronnie Jones, but the crowd didn't know that. They welcomed him to America with healthy cheers.

"It's time to Rummmmmmble in Hummmmmm-ble!"

The bell rang. Spitfire and The Annihilator circled the ring a few times stalking each other, then grabbed hold of each other around the neck. They took turns throwing the other man to the mat and performing a few other elementary wrestling moves.

It didn't take long for the serious fans in the crowd to realize that Spitfire and The Annihilator were beginners who didn't know how to put on a good show. That was the reason why they were the opening match of the night. Within a few minutes, the crowd was chanting.

"Boooooooooorrrrrrrrrrrrrrrriiiiiiinnnnnnnnggggggg!"

Both men had been instructed before the match that if the crowd reacted that way, they were to end the match quickly. The Annihilator got Spitfire in a three-quarter facelock, did a jawbreaker on him, and slammed him to the mat. When Spitfire's shoulders were down, the referee pounded his hand against the mat three times to indicate he had been pinned.

The ref held The Annihilator's hand up in the air. With some experience, both wrestlers had the potential to turn on a crowd, but not yet.

Even so, Wesley Brown was enjoying himself. His seat was right up front. His mother had given him some money to get a birthday treat, and he bought some cotton candy from a vendor who came around after Spitfire and The Annihilator left the ring.

The next match was between two wrestlers named The Nuclear Menace and Deadman. The

Nuclear Menace (usually called "Menace" for short) had a tattoo depicting an atomic explosion that filled his entire back. Deadman, according to the program, supposedly was killed in the ring several years before and came back from the dead to get revenge on the living.

In reality, both The Nuclear Menace and Deadman worked part-time in the shipping department of a Sears store. They had been wrestling around the country for several years, usually against each other.

Working so closely together, Menace and Deadman knew how to get a crowd going. Their specialty was to bounce back and forth between the ropes furiously and at the same time. Sometimes they would crash into each other. Other times one of them would stick out an arm to clothesline the other, smashing him to the mat.

Menace and Deadman had an unusual agreement. One night Menace would win, and the next fight Deadman would win. Whichever one lost would have to bleed a little. This, they decided, was fair to both men. Also, it gave the bleeder enough time to heal before he would be required to bleed again.

Many fans believe that when wrestlers bleed, it is because they have hidden mysterious "blood capsules" in their mouths and bitten down on them at the appropriate moment to make "blood" flow down their faces. That's not the way it works. When wrestlers bleed, they bleed real blood.

It was Deadman's turn to bleed on this night. A cheap folding table had been placed just outside the ring. Menace picked Deadman up and held him over his head. Then he threw Deadman over the top rope. Deadman crashed on to the table, crushing it like a house of cards. The crowd roared with approval.

Deadman lay on the floor for a full minute, the shattered table beneath him. Then he rolled over slowly onto the floor beneath the ring, where few fans could see him.

His wrist had thick tape wrapped around it, and in the folds of the tape was a tiny razor blade. Facing away from the crowd, Deadman swiped the blade gently across his forehead.

By the time Deadman climbed back into the ring, there was blood on his forehead. He smeared it around a bit, so the people in the cheaper seats would be able to see it. He appeared to be dazed and confused.

"You're a dead man, Deadman!" Menace shouted. The crowd always ate that line up, and Menace loved to deliver it.

Deadman staggered around the ring with an anguished look on his face. Menace waited until he felt the timing was right, then ran for the rope. He bounced off it, bounced to the other rope, and slammed into Deadman with a power bomb that sent Deadman to the mat. Deadman put up no resistance and Menace pinned him.

The crowd roared again as the referee held the hand of The Nuclear Menace high. Deadman limped off holding his bloody face. He would come back to life again the following week in Monroe, Indiana.

Wesley Brown was having a blast. He only wished he had a friend with him to share his birthday. Unfortunately, he and Jimmy were still mad at each other.

The next fight was a tag team match. That is, a match with two wrestlers against two other wrestlers. In this case, it was a pair of brothers called The Testosterone Twins against Mr. Kyoto and his partner Mt. Fuji. Supposedly, the Japanese team were frustrated kamikaze pilots who were angry that their nation had been at peace since the end of World War II.

In a tag team match, only one member of the team is allowed in the ring at a time. But he can tag his partner and they can switch places whenever they like.

Tag team matches are always very carefully scripted. Typically, there is one team of babyfaces (The Testosterone Twins) and another team of heels (Mr. Kyoto and Mt. Fuji). The babyfaces always start off dominating the heels. Then, just when it looks like the babyfaces are going to win, the heels cheat. One of them will grab a baseball bat or some other illegal object and whack a baby-face over the head with it.

The heels then take charge, beating the babyface in the ring mercilessly while the ref usually stands around pretending not to notice. But then the beaten babyface finds a way to get to his corner and tag his partner. The partner, enraged at the injustice of it all, beats up both heels singlehandedly. Often, a tag team match ends in a riot with all four wrestlers going at it.

The Testosterone Twins played it according to the script, finally nailing the enormous Mt. Fuji with a standing sidekick to the head and pinning him. The crowd applauded appreciatively when the ref counted the Japanese team out.

Next up was a match between two female wrestlers, Dorothy Vader and Auntie Maim. Vader, who claimed to be the long lost sister of Darth Vader, got a big pop when she came out wearing a huge black robe and waving a long fluorescent light bulb that she had fashioned into a homemade light saber using duct tape. She threw off the robe to reveal an evil-looking black bikini underneath. Auntie Maim (who used to wrestle under the name "Rosie Cheeks") could hardly compete with that. So she climbed up to the top rope and screamed insults at the crowd to attract their attention.

Neither of the women, to be honest, was very good. They had learned a few fundamental wrestling moves, but it was obvious that their hearts weren't in it. In the end, the match was reduced to slapping and hair pulling. Still, most people in the crowd had never seen two women beating each other up, and the novelty of it held their attention. Both ladies received a standing ovation when it was over. Auntie Maim was the winner.

The crowd barely had time to sit back in their seats when the next match began. From the ready room emerged a wrestler who called himself Fear. He had one of the strangest gimmicks in all of wrestling. Fear was a frustrated actor who would quote famous sayings as he wrestled.

"The only thing we have to fear," he announced to the crowd after climbing into the ring, "is Fear itself!"

Fear carried a copy of *Bartlett's Familiar Quotations* with him at all times, even in the middle of a fight. It wasn't quite clear if Fear was supposed to be a heel or a babyface, but pretty much everyone hated him.

Usually Fear was matched against an obviously dumb guy. On this night his opponent was a wrestler named Half Brain. His story was that he was so violent, he had half his brain removed to calm him down. Some people even claimed that Half Brain was born with *no* brain.

The truth was, he had a fully functional brain, and used it to run three Burger King restaurants in Kalamazoo, Michigan.

Fear got the upper hand in the match right away and began pummeling Half Brain.

"Thirty days has September," he shouted. "When I'm done, you'll be dismembered!"

Half Brain lay semiconscious at the edge of the ring. Fear got up on the top rope and leaped off, landing on Half Brain.

"That's one small step for man," he hollered, "one giant leap on your butt!"

Fear took his copy of *Bartlett's Familiar Quotations* and began hitting Half Brain over the head with it. That got the crowd very angry. Half Brain, was, after all, mentally handicapped.

"Ask not what your country can do for you," Fear yelled to Half Brain's lifeless form. "Ask what a good doctor can do for you."

Suddenly, out of the ready room charged The Nuclear Menace, Deadman, and Auntie Maim. They attacked Fear as a group and beat the snot out of him. While they were doing that, Half Brain struggled to his feet just in time to be declared the winner by the ref. The crowd went nuts.

There was a short intermission at that point, and many of the fans took the opportunity to use the rest room or buy refreshments. Wesley was relaxing in his seat when there was a tap on his shoulder. It was his mother.

"What are you doing here, Mom?"

"I thought it over and decided you were right,"

she said. "If I'm going to protest against something, I should see it with my own eyes."

She took the seat next to Wesley just as the ring announcer came out.

"And now, ladies and gentlemen, it is time for our main event of the evening. In this corner, weighing so many pounds that no existing scale can possibly measure him, the amazing . . . Subhuman Newman!"

Subhuman Newman was an enormous bald man wearing a loin cloth. He had a big turkey leg in one hand and a stapler in the other. He took a bite out of the turkey. Then he took the stapler and clicked it repeatedly against his arm. Wesley and his mom could actually *see* the staples in his arm.

"That's disgusting!" Bonnie Brown said, but Wesley couldn't hear her because the crowd reaction was so loud.

"And in this corner," the ring announcer continued when the noise level dropped a bit, "weighing 250 pounds! Born and raised by wolves in Death Valley, Nevada, the lowest spot in North America. It's the lowest, dirtiest *man* in North America. The one. The only. Doctor . . . Demented!"

"Booooooooooooooooooo!"

"Yeeeeaaaaahhhhhhh!"

Wesley cheered uncontrollably when Mr. Wheeler came in wearing his Dr. Demented costume.

"How can you root for somebody named Doctor Demented?" Bonnie Brown asked, covering her ears.

"He's the greatest!" Wesley replied.

"I . . . RULE . . . THIS . . . PATHETIC . . . WORLD!" Dr. Demented bellowed, with the entire crowd shouting right along with him.

Subhuman Newman didn't just stand around while Dr. Demented drank in the crowd reaction. He jumped out of the ring and grabbed a metal folding chair from the front row. Then he climbed back into the ring, snuck up behind Dr. Demented, and slammed the chair over his head. Dr. Demented collapsed to the mat.

"Wesley! He just hit Doctor Demented with a chair!" Bonnie Brown exclaimed.

"Yeah, wasn't that cool?"

"Don't they have rules?"

"Sure they do," Wesley informed his mother. "Chair shots are perfectly legal."

Subhuman Newman tossed away the dented chair and marched around the ring triumphantly, celebrating his accomplishment. Dr. Demented shook his head, as if to clear the cobwebs away.

"Why do you want to see one man hit another man over the head with a chair?" Bonnie asked Wesley.

"They're collapsible chairs, Mom!"

"I don't care if they're papier-mâché. Why do you want to see that?"

"It's fun!" Wesley replied. "It must be a guy thing."

"It's a *sick* thing."

Dr. Demented finally got up off the mat. He must not have been hurt very badly, because he went after Subhuman Newman with a vengeance. The two of them went through a series of complicated maneuvers that had the crowd spellbound. Top rope cross body blocks. German suplex. Twisting dives. Firebird splashes.

These men were professionals, and they knew how to put on a show. Dr. Demented had the upper hand for a few minutes, and then Subhuman Newman dominated the match for the next few minutes. It was a seesaw battle.

"Ugh. This is even worse than I thought it would be," Bonnie Brown said in the middle of it all. "Let's get out of here."

"Mom! It's my birthday present!"

Wesley's mother only saw the violence. She failed to grasp the beauty or psychology of wrestling.

Dr. Demented was a master psychologist. He knew how to convincingly hit a man without actually hurting him. He was an expert at getting hit, too, staggering backward from the force of a blow to make it look real. He knew exactly how long to lie on the mat in order to gain the crowd's sympathy, and how slowly he should struggle to his feet and regain his senses.

He knew how to pace a ten-minute fight to bring the crowd's emotions up and down like a roller coaster ride. His timing was perfect. Every time Subhuman Newman knocked him down, he would get up just *a little* more slowly to show the crowd the beating was taking a toll on his body.

For a serious wrestling fan, watching Dr. Demented in action was like watching a ballet. A very violent ballet.

At the nine-minute mark, Dr. Demented had taken control of the match. Subhuman Newman was lying in the center of the ring, unable to stand up. The crowd was screaming for a quick pin.

But Dr. Demented wouldn't give it to them. Instead, he hopped out of the ring and ran to the side of the arena. There was a ten-foot ladder there. Dr. Demented picked it up and carried it back to the ring with him.

"He's gonna do it!" Wesley shouted in his mother's ear.

"Do what? Hit him with that ladder?"

"No, his signature move," Wesley replied. "The Doctor Demented Death Drop."

"What's that?"

"You'll see."

Dr. Demented positioned the ladder about five feet from Subhuman Newman, who was struggling to get up. Then he climbed to the top of the ladder.

"I . . . RULE . . . THIS . . . PATHETIC . . . WORLD!" Dr. Demented shouted. Then he leaped off the ladder, flew through the air, and landed on top of Subhuman Newman with a thud. The ref was right there, hitting the floor three times to show that Newman was pinned.

The roar of the crowd was deafening. As Dr. Demented ran past Wesley and his mother on the way to the ready room, he tossed Wesley a wink. The house lights came on and people gathered up their coats to go. Wesley used his own money to buy a souvenir program on the way out.

"Thanks, Mom," Wesley said in the car on the way home. "That was the best birthday present I ever had."

Bonnie Brown drove for a while wordlessly, trying to understand what she had just witnessed. She couldn't figure out why anyone would want to watch such violence. What did it say about American society? What did it say about her own son? Would Wesley grow up to be like his father? Would he be hitting somebody like that someday?

And why did that awful Dr. Demented guy wink at Wesley?

17

Instant Muscles

WESLEY WAS MORE THAN A LITTLE SURPRISED the day after the wrestling match when his doorbell rang and Jimmy Erdman was standing on the porch. Wesley hadn't spoken to Jimmy since their argument a week before, when Carl Campanella set Wesley's shoes on fire and Jimmy didn't do anything to stop it.

"What do *you* want?" Wesley asked cautiously through the screen door. He didn't want to act too nice to Jimmy, but at the same time, he didn't want to look like he wouldn't accept an apology if Jimmy was offering one.

"I came to say I was sorry, man," Jimmy said. "I should have stood up to Campanella."

"Forget it," Wesley said, relieved. He didn't like arguments. When you only have one true friend, you have to be careful how you treat him. Both Wesley and Jimmy knew that.

"Hey, I brought you a birthday present," Jimmy

said, holding up a little box he had wrapped in the Sunday comics.

"What is it?"

"It's kinda private," Jimmy said, looking around to see if Wesley's mother was nearby. "Let's go to your room."

As they pounded up the steps, Wesley told Jimmy excitedly about the wrestling match. It turned out that Jimmy had been there, too, with his dad.

"Wasn't it cool when Doctor Demented did the Death Drop?" Jimmy asked.

"Yeah, that was awesome!"

"Maybe Mr. Wheeler would teach us how to do that."

"I doubt it."

The boys went into Wesley's room and shut the door.

"So what's the big secret?" Wesley asked.

Jimmy handed him the box.

"Go ahead," he said. "Open it."

Wesley ripped off the wrapping paper and opened up the box about the size of a Band-Aid box. Inside the box was a plastic bottle. It said "ANDROS-TENEDIONE" on it. Wesley shook the container. There were pills inside.

"What's this stuff?" he asked. "Some kind of crea-tine?"

"No, it's andro," Jimmy replied. "This is the stuff that Mark McGwire took that year he hit seventy home runs. This stuff makes creatine look like Flintstone vitamins."

Wesley read the label on the bottle.

Androstenedione is a natural steroid alternative found in all animals and some plants. Our product has been scientifically proven to increase testosterone levels by nearly 300% within two hours. It will give you increased energy, quicker recovery from exercise, enhanced muscle growth, as well as greater sense of well-being. Our product has been HPLC tested for 100% purity. We guarantee it to be the purest and most potent androstenedione available.

"What's HPLC?" Wesley asked.

"I don't know. It must be a lab or something."

"Is this stuff safe?"

"I bought it in the health food store," Jimmy explained. "It must be healthy for you, right?"

"I don't know . . ."

"Wes, it's instant muscles. All the bodybuilders take it."

Wesley had been working out faithfully for over a month. He didn't have any muscles to show for it yet. He twisted the childproof cap off the bottle. The pills were small and yellow.

"Go ahead, take one," Jimmy urged.

Wesley popped the little pill into his mouth.

"Happy birthday," Jimmy said as Wesley gulped the pill down.

18

A Big Mistake

WHEN THE HUMBLE CIVIC CENTER WASN'T hosting professional wrestling, it hosted a series of classical music concerts titled "Mostly Mozart." Bonnie Brown was a subscriber to the series and she tried to catch all the concerts. A few of her former students actually played in the orchestra, and she was very proud of them.

Wesley had never been to one of the concerts, and his mother was always trying to get him to go. She had a good reason. She wanted something to compensate for the negative influence of all those wrestling matches he watched on TV. Bonnie figured that if Wesley was exposed to the beauty of classical music, maybe it would make up for those nights of watching a bunch of sweaty men in shorts beat each other up. Logical or not, it couldn't hurt to give him a little culture, she figured.

Wesley hated classical music, but he agreed to go to Mostly Mozart even though his mother forced him to wear his nice pants and a button-down shirt. He agreed to go because Mr. Wheeler was going with them. It was the first time Wesley's mom and Mr. Wheeler had invited him to join them on a date. Wesley couldn't resist the chance to see his mom out on the town with Dr. Demented.

Landon Wheeler showed up with flowers hidden behind his back, as usual. He was wearing a suit and tie. Wesley's mom was all giggly when Mr. Wheeler gave her the flowers, like she was a schoolgirl or something. She never acted like that normally. She even gave Mr. Wheeler a kiss in front of Wesley.

When they walked into the Humble Civic Center, Wesley hoped he wouldn't see anybody from school. Everybody already thought he was a nerd. If word got around that he went to Mozart concerts, there was no telling what might happen.

They settled into their seats, with Bonnie sitting between Wesley and Mr. Wheeler. The music started. Minuet from Divertimento in D Major, according to the program. It was actually sort of pleasant, Wesley thought. He wouldn't want to get the CD or anything, but at least it wasn't elevator music.

The nice thing about classical music, Wesley decided, was that you didn't have to pay attention to it. He looked around the Humble Civic Center, amazed at how quiet everyone was. During the wrestling show, the crowd was screaming and pounding the floor with their feet the whole time. Here, they were sitting in their fancy dresses with their hands folded neatly in their laps and watching silently.

Wesley glanced at his mom and noticed that she was holding hands with Mr. Wheeler. It threw him a little. Of course he understood that they had been going out for a while now and would be expected to hold hands. But up until that point, they hadn't put on any PDAs—public displays of affection. It made Wesley feel a little strange.

At the wrestling show, Dr. Demented had been on stage beating the guy to a pulp. Here, he was sitting in the audience with an angelic look on his face and holding hands with Wesley's mother while a guy played a violin. *Too weird.*

After a while Wesley noticed that his eyelids were closing. He found himself fighting to keep them open. Fortunately, the orchestra stopped playing and the audience broke into applause. People began getting up from their seats.

"Is it over?" Wesley asked.

"Intermission," his mother explained.

"I've got to go to the little boy's room," Mr. Wheeler announced. "How about you, Wesley?"

"Sure." Anything to get out of his seat and move his legs a little.

They passed the concession stand on the way to the men's room and Mr. Wheeler offered to buy Wesley a T-shirt with Wolfgang Amadeus Mozart's face on it. Wesley had noticed that the longer his mom went out with Mr. Wheeler, the more attention Mr. Wheeler paid to him.

They were nice T-shirts. Wesley thought it over, ultimately deciding that if somebody like Carl Campanella ever saw Wesley wearing a Mozart T-shirt, he would probably set it on fire or throw it down the sewer or something.

"No thanks, Mr. Wheeler," Wesley said diplomatically, "I have too many T-shirts as it is."

"Wes, I think maybe it's time you called me Landon instead of Mr. Wheeler when we're not at school. Would that be okay with you?"

"Uh, sure, Mr. . . . uh, Landon. Why?"

"Well, your mom and I are getting close, and I'm beginning to feel funny when you call me Mr. Wheeler."

"Close?" Wesley asked. "What does that mean? Close to what?"

"Wes," Mr. Wheeler said seriously. "I think I'm in love with your mother."

Wesley gulped. He knew they liked each other. He knew they liked each other *a lot*. But love? That's *serious*.

"Does she feel the same way about you?"

"I don't know," Mr. Wheeler replied. "I hope so. I haven't told her yet."

Wesley walked into the men's room in a daze. Having a guy in love with his mother would take some getting used to.

The bathroom was jammed with men and there were only a few urinals. Everybody stood around waiting, and whenever a urinal was free, somebody would step forward to use it. There was no real line. Guys would just make eye contact with each other and gesture for the other guy to take his turn.

A urinal opened up and Mr. Wheeler told Wesley to take it. He did. When he was done, Mr. Wheeler stepped forward to take his turn.

"Hey, I was here first, buddy," a guy in a blue suit said.

Mr. Wheeler turned around before he got to the urinal. The guy in the blue suit was *big*. He wasn't quite as muscular as Mr. Wheeler, but he was a few inches taller.

"I beg your pardon?" Mr. Wheeler asked.

"I said it's my turn."

"Then by all means, sir, take your turn," Mr. Wheeler said, gesturing toward the urinal.

"You bein' smart with me?" the guy in the blue suit snapped.

Landon Wheeler was used to guys like this. Every so often a guy would come up to him and pick a fight. Usually they wanted to impress their friends or date with how tough they were by picking a fight with a really big guy. Sometimes they were just drunk. Landon Wheeler knew the best way to handle a guy like that was to back away. Fighting guys was something he did for his job, not in his spare time.

"It's all yours," Mr. Wheeler said politely.

But the guy in the blue suit didn't go to the urinal. He stepped toward Mr. Wheeler.

"I think you're bein' smart with me, fella."

"I assure you, I'm not."

"Why don't you just do your business?" a voice in the back complained.

"Nobody talks smart to me," the guy said, advancing on Mr. Wheeler. "Why don't you and I step outside?"

"I'd rather not," Mr. Wheeler said, retreating to the line of sinks.

"Then we'll settle it right here," the guy said, pushing Mr. Wheeler on the chest with both hands.

"You're making a big mistake," Mr. Wheeler told the guy. "Please don't do this. For your own sake."

"I'll do whatever I want," the guy replied. He made a fist with his right hand and brought it back to throw a punch.

Mr. Wheeler caught the punch with his hand before it could reach his head. With his other hand, he threw a quick jab that hit the guy in the stomach. The guy doubled over from the force of the blow and fell forward, smacking his head on a sink on the way down. He groaned once, then closed his eyes and fell silent. Mr. Wheeler cursed in disgust.

"Serves the guy right," somebody muttered.

"Get a doctor," Mr. Wheeler instructed.

"Wow!" Wesley exclaimed. "You punched that guy's lights out!"

Within seconds, word spread throughout the arena about the fight in the men's rest room. Several doctors in the audience rushed to lend assistance. An ambulance siren could be heard. Two police officers arrived to ask questions of anyone who witnessed the altercation.

"We never had any problems with the *wrestling* crowd," one of the cops commented when he walked into the rest room.

When she heard that there had been a fight in the men's bathroom, Bonnie Brown rushed over to see what was happening.

"Are you okay?" she asked, throwing her arms around Wesley protectively.

"You should have seen it, Mom!" Wesley said. "This jerk started hassling Mr. Wheeler, and he flattened the guy with one punch! It was cool!"

Bonnie looked at Mr. Wheeler, horrified.

"You *hit* somebody?" she asked, disbelieving.

"It wasn't his fault, Mom!" Wesley said, before Mr. Wheeler could answer. "The guy hit him first. Mr. Wheeler was just defending himself."

"I can't believe you had to resort to *violence*,"

Bonnie said disgustedly. "Surely you could have resolved the problem another way."

"Bonnie," Mr. Wheeler protested, "you don't understand. Sometimes guys want to pick a fight—"

"Take us home!" Bonnie ordered.

"The piano concerto is next," Mr. Wheeler protested.

"Fine," Bonnie said, walking out the lobby. "You stay for the piano concerto. Wesley and I will take a taxi."

Mr. Wheeler hurried after her like a lost puppy. There were no PDAs in the car on the way home. Wesley's mother didn't say a word to Mr. Wheeler. When he dropped them off, she didn't say good-bye. And she didn't give him a kiss either.

19

Get Ripped

AFTER TAKING ANDROSTENEDIONE FOR A few days, Wesley began to feel an unusual sensation in his chest and shoulders. He couldn't exactly say what the feeling was. He couldn't see that his muscles were any bigger when he looked in the mirror. But he felt like his body was stronger. He felt like the pills might be actually *doing* something in there.

When he went over to Mr. Wheeler's garage for his next workout, Wesley decided to add ten pounds to his weights. If he was truly stronger now, he figured, he should be able to lift a little more weight than what it said on the weight training chart Mr. Wheeler had designed for him. The more he could lift, the bigger his muscles would become.

Besides, it made him feel better about himself that he could pick up those ten extra pounds. Mr.

Wheeler had started him off with so little weight, he felt like he wasn't picking up much more than the bar itself.

Mr. Wheeler didn't seem to be paying close attention, so Wesley slipped the extra weight on his barbell.

"I feel terrible about what happened at the concert," Mr. Wheeler lamented as Wesley went though his barbell curls. "Your mother was really furious at me."

"Don't worry about it," Wesley assured him. "Mom gets mad at me all the time."

"Do you think she'll forgive me?"

"Sure she will."

Man, grown-ups are weird, Wesley thought to himself. The great Dr. Demented can dominate any man. But as soon as a woman gets angry at him, he collapses like a week-old party balloon.

Mr. Wheeler went off to do something in the kitchen and Wesley went through his exercise routine. The ten extra pounds required a little extra effort than he was used to. He had to grunt a bit to get the weight up. It was a struggle, but he did it.

Wesley was doing side laterals with a dumbbell in each hand when he felt a searing pain shoot through his left shoulder. It felt like something ripped in there, like he had been stabbed. He knew that he didn't have the strength to hold a toothpick, much less a dumbbell.

The dumbbells slipped from his hands and clanged

against the floor. Wesley grabbed his left shoulder with his right arm and bent over in pain. Mr. Wheeler heard the noise and came running from the kitchen.

"What happened?" he asked.

"Something ripped," Wesley said, grimacing to get the words out while fighting back tears. "In my shoulder."

"Sounds like a torn rotator cuff."

Mr. Wheeler ran to get some ice and used a dish towel to make an ice pack. The cold made Wesley's shoulder hurt even more, but he knew ice was good for just about all sports injuries. When Wesley had calmed down a little, Mr. Wheeler looked at the dumbbell on the floor.

"You've got too much weight here," he said. "Why were you using these?"

Wesley could have lied. He could have explained that it was a mistake. He could say he had no idea he had accidentally picked up the wrong dumbbells.

But Wesley had never been a good liar, and he didn't think this would be a good time to start.

"I thought I could lift more weight," he admitted, wincing.

"What made you think that?" Mr. Wheeler asked.

"Well, I've been taking this stuff," he said, pulling the bottle out of his pocket, "and it made me feel stronger."

"You're on *andro*?" Mr. Wheeler asked, his eyes popping out. Wesley shrank back in terror. Mr. Wheeler had the look in his eyes that he got just before he finished off one of his opponents in the ring.

"I'm sorry!"

"Wesley this is powerful stuff! It's not for kids."

"I was stupid," Wesley admitted. "I just wanted to get ripped, like you."

"Like *me*? I wouldn't *touch* this stuff," Mr. Wheeler declared, taking the bottle from Wesley's hand. "A lot of scientists say andro causes heart disease, pancreatic cancer, and strokes."

Mr. Wheeler opened the bottle and dumped the remaining pills into a trash can in the corner of the garage. He shook his head from side to side, angry at himself even more than he was angry at Wesley. Up until this point, he'd thought Wesley merely wanted to get in shape. Now he realized that Wesley was becoming obsessed with his body image.

"Wes," he said more calmly. "You don't need that stuff. You're a great kid. People are going to like you for you, not because you have big muscles. Just be yourself."

"Be *yourself*?" Now it was Wesley's turn to be angry. "Look at *you*. Every week you put on a costume that hides your face and you pretend to be somebody who's nothing like you. And you're telling me that *I* should be myself?"

Landon Wheeler had never thought about that. He was stunned.

"Let's take you home," he said quietly.

Mr. Wheeler put another towel around the ice bag to secure it on Wesley's shoulder and walked him down the street.

"Please don't tell my mom about the andro," Wesley begged as they reached the front door to his house. "She'll kill me."

"She won't kill you."

"I didn't tell her *your* secret," Wesley pointed out. "Please don't tell her mine."

Mr. Wheeler couldn't argue with that. The whole time he had been dating Wesley's mom, Wesley had not said a word to her about his secret life as Dr. Demented.

"We'll just tell her the truth—you hurt your shoulder lifting weight," Mr. Wheeler said, ringing the doorbell.

It was a good thing they didn't mention the andro to Bonnie Brown. Just hearing that Wesley had injured himself lifting weights made her furious.

"I *never* should have let him do this weight lifting foolishness in the first place," she hissed when Mr. Wheeler told her what had happened. "Look what you did to him!"

"I'm sorry, Bonnie," Mr. Wheeler sputtered meekly. "I accept full responsibility."

"That won't fix my son's shoulder!"

"It's not Mr. Wheeler's fault," Wesley explained to his mother. "It's my fault. I tried to lift too much weight."

Bonnie Brown wasn't buying it. "Can't you see he's a thinker?" she asked Mr. Wheeler, wrapping her arms around Wesley. "Why do you muscleheads have to try to make young boys feel like they need to look like you? Can't you see that it's his *brain* that's going to develop rather than his body?"

"I'm sorry," Mr. Wheeler repeated. There was nothing else he could say.

"Look," she said, pointing a finger at him. "I don't want Wesley seeing you anymore. And I don't want to see you anymore either."

20

Bad News

WESLEY'S SHOULDER INJURY WAS NOT A total tear, just a badly strained muscle. If he stopped lifting weights and gave it a lot of rest, the doctor told him, the shoulder would heal up just fine.

But the strain on the relationship between Bonnie Brown and Mr. Wheeler would not heal so easily. Bonnie felt very strongly about Landon, but she couldn't get past the fact that he would hit somebody over whose turn it was to use the bathroom.

Landon Wheeler didn't get to be the four-time AWF champion by being a quitter. When Bonnie informed him that she didn't want to see him anymore, he began planning his campaign to win her back.

First came the flowers. Bunches of them, delivered every day. Then he sent over chocolates and helium balloons that said I'M SORRY on them. Love letters appeared in her mailbox, begging for forgiveness.

There was no response. When he tried to call and talk things over, she hung up on him.

Mr. Wheeler composed poems and stuck them under the windshield wiper of Bonnie's car before she left for work in the morning. One night she came home to see the words I LOVE YOU written in huge letters with sidewalk chalk on the driveway. She washed it off with the hose.

Wesley and Jimmy were throwing a Frisbee in the street in front of Wesley's house after school one day. The mailman drove his truck down the street and Mr. Wheeler ran out of his house to intercept it. Jimmy and Wesley watched as Mr. Wheeler handed the mailman—also a big guy— some money.

"What's he doing?" Jimmy asked.

"Beats me."

The mailman took a uniform out of his truck and Mr. Wheeler put it on over his T-shirt and shorts. Then he went over to Wesley's house and rang the doorbell. When Bonnie opened the door, he got down on his knees and put his hands together like he was praying. She closed the door in his face.

"Don't look now," Jimmy told Wesley, "but Doctor Demented is weeping on your front porch."

Nothing Mr. Wheeler did changed Bonnie's mind. He wasn't used to failure. Sadness began to show in his face. It seemed to be affecting his entire life.

Most days, in phys ed, Mr. Wheeler organized games, led exercises, and talked to the boys about the importance of good nutrition. But ever since the incident at the concert, he would just hand out a bunch of basketballs and tell the boys to go shoot hoops. Then he would retreat into his office.

Wesley had been ordered by the doctor not to play ball because of his shoulder. He knocked on Mr. Wheeler's door at the back of the gym.

"Are you okay?" he asked when Mr. Wheeler let him in.

"Yeah, I guess I'm just a little down over what happened with your mom," he replied. "I've tried everything I can think of to make her forgive me."

"My mom can be tough sometimes."

"You know her better than anyone," Mr. Wheeler submitted. "Can you think of anything I could do to get her back? What do *you* do when she's angry at you?"

"I usually hide in my room until she gets over it."

"That won't do me any good. She won't even let me in the front door."

"Well, she loves music. . . ."

The next morning, Mr. Wheeler was outside Bonnie's window, strumming a guitar and singing "You . . . are . . . so . . . beautiful . . . to me . . ."

"Mom, what's your problem?" Wesley asked when she turned on the radio to drown out the sound. "Mr. Wheeler is in love with you. How can you ignore him like this?"

"He told you that?"

"Yes! The poor guy loves you so much he's humiliating himself out there for you. Doesn't that mean anything?"

"Of course it does," Bonnie said. "But I can't get that incident at the concert out of my mind. You know how I feel about violence."

"It wasn't Mr. Wheeler's fault!" Wesley insisted. "That creep was looking to start a fight. He was probably drunk."

"So every time some drunk decides to challenge him to a fight, he's got to punch the guy? I don't want to be with a man like that."

"Mom, he said it will never happen again."

"This whole bodybuilding thing makes me uncomfortable," Bonnie complained. "You see what happens? I'm suspicious of anyone, male or female, who invests so much energy into making themselves look good. Having big muscles just shouldn't be so important."

"But, Mom, do you love him?"

Bonnie Brown didn't answer.

* * *

After school the next day, Wesley told his mother he was going over to Jimmy's house to play computer games. It was a lie. He went over to Mr. Wheeler's house instead.

"How's the shoulder?" Mr. Wheeler asked when he saw it was Wesley at the door.

"Getting better."

"Wesley, I thought you weren't allowed over here."

"I'm not," Wesley replied. "I was worried about you. You seem so depressed lately."

Mr. Wheeler let Wesley in and sat down heavily on the couch.

"I've got a lot on my mind."

"I came over to tell you something," Wesley said, taking the chair. "I think my mom really loves you. I asked her if she did, and she wouldn't give me an answer. So I figure she must love you, because if she didn't love you she would have said so."

"Wesley, it's not just about your mother."

"What do you mean?"

"I received a letter today," Mr. Wheeler explained, pulling a piece of paper out of his pocket. "It's the script for my fight next week. It's at the Astrodome again. Are you going to be there?"

"Nah," Wesley said. "There's no way my mom would let me go. But Jimmy said his dad has tickets."

"It's probably just as well that you don't go. It

looks like the AWF is trying to drum up some publicity. So they're going to announce in advance that if Dr. Demented loses the match, he's going to take off his mask in front of the whole crowd."

"Unmask you?" Wesley said with a gasp.

"Yeah. Not only that. It also says . . . I'm going to job."

"Job?" Wesley was incredulous. "You can't job! Doctor Demented never loses."

"I'm an employee of the AWF, and if they say I'm going to job, I job. They call the shots. I guess the AWF has had enough of my character. Probably the Doctor Demented T-shirts aren't selling the way they used to."

"I can't believe it!" Wesley exclaimed. "Does that mean your career is over?"

"They may want to turn me into a face."

"A babyface?" Again, Wesley was flabbergasted. "You? You make such a great heel!"

"I know. I *created* Doctor Demented. It almost feels like he's a part of me. I had such a good thing going, teaching during the day and wrestling on weekends. I knew this day would come. I just thought I would be out of wrestling before they decided to kill off Doctor Demented."

"What are you gonna do?"

"I can't take off my mask," Mr. Wheeler lamented. "The school board will fire me if they find out I'm a professional wrestler."

"Won't the AWF fire you if you don't follow their script?"

"Yes."

"So no matter what you do, one of them is going to fire you."

"That's right."

21

Friends Help Friends

"GIVE ME THE SHOES, MOUSE," CARL CAM-
panella said with a smirk.

Most grown-ups had a theory about why Carl
Campanella was only happy when he was making
other people unhappy. It had to be his miserable
childhood, they'd say. He must have been neg-
lected. His parents probably didn't love him.
Maybe they beat him. Or his older brother tor-
tured him. Who knew? Maybe there was a "jerk"
gene, and Carl inherited it.

But when he was in your face giving you a hard
time, none of those things mattered.

Wesley did his best to avoid Carl Campanella. If
he saw Carl coming his way at school, he would
duck down a hallway and walk far out of his way
so he wouldn't have to cross paths with him. Carl
knew it. That's why he enjoyed hassling Wesley so
much.

Wesley didn't look up right away when Carl said, "Give me the shoes, Mouse." He was sick of Carl Campanella. What was Campanella's problem, anyway? Couldn't his family afford new shoes?

Phys ed had been over for ten minutes, but a lot of the boys were still milling around the locker room. Wesley was down on one knee tying his left shoe. The right one was still untied.

He thought of his alternatives. He could just hand over the shoes to Campanella and be done with it. But he'd look like a wimp. And it wouldn't be the end of it. Campanella would probably bother him for something else.

He could make a run for it. But Campanella would eventually catch up with him.

He could refuse to give Campanella anything and see what he would do. But Carl might do something violent.

He could call for Mr. Wheeler, whose office was not far from the locker room. But then he would be the laughingstock of the school, running for a grown-up to fight his battles for him.

For a brief moment Wesley thought about taking off one shoe and slamming it into Carl Campanella's head, heel first. That would wipe the smirk off Carl's face. But it wasn't Wesley's nature to be violent.

"My name is *Wes*," he said, rising to face Campanella. "Not Mouse."

Wesley still wasn't sure what he was going to do. He wasn't sure he had the guts to stand up to Campanella, but if he was going to give up his shoes, he wanted to keep at least some of his dignity.

"I don't care what your name is," Carl Campanella said. "Hand over the shoes."

A crowd started to gather around, as it usually did when it seemed like two boys were going to fight.

"Why?" Wesley asked.

Carl Campanella was not used to backtalk. He liked his victims to give in without a fight, as losers should to a true conquering hero. He made a fist with his right hand, just in case he would need to use it.

"Because if you don't, Mouse, I'm gonna knock your teeth in."

Wesley's eyes darted across the boys gathered behind Campanella. He couldn't count on any of them for help. He was looking for Jimmy but couldn't find him. Jimmy was probably hiding, Wesley thought bitterly.

But Jimmy wasn't hiding this time. When he heard Carl start hassling Wesley, Jimmy snuck around the next row of lockers. He slid the wooden bench over to a locker and climbed up on it. Carefully putting a foot into the empty locker, Jimmy hoisted his huge body up until he was on top of the row of lockers.

Jimmy was afraid his weight might bend the cheap metal, but it held. He peeked over the edge until he saw the back of Carl Campanella's head. Jimmy moved six inches over, until he was directly above Campanella.

"I'm gonna give you one last chance, Mouse," Campanella was saying. "Don't force me to hurt you."

That's when Carl Campanella pulled out a knife. It was a little pocket knife, but it was a real knife and it was sharp.

From his angle above the lockers, Jimmy couldn't see the knife.

Wesley certainly saw the knife. He wasn't about to risk getting stabbed over a pair of shoes. Without taking his eyes off Campanella, Wesley slid off his right shoe and used his right foot to force the left shoe off his left foot.

"Take 'em," Wesley said, kicking the shoes over to Campanella.

"That's a good boy," Campanella said. "Do as you're told."

As Campanella bent down to pick up the shoes, Jimmy stood up on top of the lockers. Every boy in the locker room saw him. Every boy except Carl Campanella.

Jimmy launched himself off the locker like he was cannonballing into a swimming pool, his arms outstretched. All one hundred and fifty pounds of dead weight hurtled through the air, his backside hitting Campanella flush across the shoulder blades. Campanella crumpled to the floor, his knife clattering away harmlessly.

"I rule your pathetic world, Campanella!" Jimmy proclaimed upon impact.

Carl Campanella didn't hear it. He was unconscious the instant his head slammed against the locker. In a way, that was fortunate for him. When his left arm fractured between the elbow and wrist, Carl didn't feel a thing.

Campanella's body served to cushion Jimmy's fall somewhat, but not completely. Jimmy bounced off and landed on the hard concrete floor. His right knee struck the floor first, shattering the kneecap. Jimmy had never felt so much pain in his life.

"What's going on in here?" boomed the voice of Mr. Wheeler at the other end of the locker room.

The freshman boys were usually pretty rowdy in the locker room, and Mr. Wheeler didn't like to come in unless there was an emergency. But when he heard the words "I rule your pathetic world!" he had to see what was happening.

The boys who had been standing around watching Carl and Wesley scurried back to their lockers and pretended to be busy. Carl Campanella lay in a heap, facedown on the floor. Jimmy lay on his back next to Carl, holding his knee.

"Man, that was beautiful!" Wesley told Jimmy. "You're crazy! Why'd you do that?"

"Friends help friends," Jimmy grimaced through

the pain. "I felt bad about last time. I just wish I coulda seen the look on Campanella's face when I nailed him."

Mr. Wheeler rushed over and saw the two boys lying on the floor.

"What happened?" he asked Wesley, reaching for the cell phone in his back pocket.

"Carl pulled a knife on me . . ." Wesley explained.

Jimmy thought Wesley was making the story up to get him off the hook, but Wesley picked the knife off the floor and handed it to Mr. Wheeler.

". . . so Jimmy climbed on top of the lockers and jumped on him. Jimmy's a hero, Mr. Wheeler."

"I need an ambulance over to the gym at Nimitz High School," Mr. Wheeler barked into the phone.

Mr. Wheeler checked to make sure that Carl Campanella was breathing, then he turned his attention to Jimmy.

"Is it your knee?" Mr. Wheeler asked, holding Jimmy's leg out straight.

"Yeah."

"I know you were trying to protect Wes, but that wasn't a very smart thing to do, Jimmy. Where'd you get that idea?"

"From Doctor Demented," Jimmy replied honestly.

Mr. Wheeler looked horrified.

22

The Decision

LANDON WHEELER GUNNED HIS SPORTS car up route 610 heading for the Astrodome. Usually, he used his driving time to rehearse in his mind the moves he was going to be performing in the ring.

Not today. The AWF hadn't even informed him who his opponent was going to be. He didn't really care. He had other things on his mind.

Two miles from the Astrodome, Landon Wheeler still hadn't reached a decision about the letter he had received from the AWF. If he jobbed the match and took off the Dr. Demented mask, he could kiss his teaching job good-bye. And if he disobeyed AWF orders and didn't follow the script, he could kiss his professional wrestling career good-bye. Nobody wants to hire a guy who doesn't follow directions.

Landon Wheeler *was* sure of one thing. He was

deeply disturbed after seeing what happened when Jimmy Erdman imitated his "Doctor Demented Death Drop" on Carl Campanella. What if Carl had smashed his head on the concrete floor? What if his skull had been fractured? What if he had died?

Landon was so wrapped up in these thoughts that he almost missed the turnoff for the Astrodome. As he pulled into the front gate, a few fans were already there, holding tailgate parties in the parking lot.

Meanwhile, Wesley Brown couldn't believe his rotten luck. Here it was, the night of the most important match in professional wrestling history. This was the night Dr. Demented might—or might not—lose for the first time and be forced to remove his mask. And *he* was sitting home doing nothing. It wasn't fair.

Wesley could have gotten free tickets from Mr. Wheeler. But he knew his mom would never let him use them.

Jimmy was so lucky, Wesley thought bitterly. *His* parents took him to drag races, monster truck pulls, R rated movies, anything he wanted. They didn't care how much violence Jimmy was exposed to.

Wesley glanced up at the clock. The first match would begin in less than an hour. He picked up one of his wrestling magazines and thumbed through it.

The phone rang. He recognized Jimmy's voice right away.

"You in the car?" Wesley asked. "Are you calling to rub it in that you're there and I'm not?"

"No, I'm home," Jimmy replied.

"What are you doing home? You're going to be late for the match!"

"I just got back from the doctor's office. They shot an MRI. The doctor took one look at it and said I can't go."

"Not even on crutches?"

"Nope. I have to keep my leg elevated."

"Can't they get you a wheelchair or something?"

"It's too late."

"That stinks!"

"Don't I know it," Jimmy agreed. "Look, Wes, I know your mom probably won't let you go, but I thought I'd offer you the tickets anyway. They're ringside."

Wesley looked at the clock again. There was no way he could get to the Astrodome on time. He would have to miss the preliminary matches. But he could get there in time for the main event. The wheels began turning in his head.

"Hold on," Wesley said into the phone. "Uh, Mom, can I talk to you about something?"

"What is it?" Bonnie Brown asked.

"Jimmy just got back from the doctor," Wesley blurted, "and the doctor won't let him go to the wrestling match and he's got ringside seats and he wants me to have them and I really want to go because it's a really important match and it means so much to me and can't we go, please, please, *please*?"

"No," Bonnie Brown said simply.

"But, Mom, I promise you I will never ask for anything else for the rest of my life!"

"No."

"Mom, I promise I'll never go see wrestling again. Ever. *Pleeeaaase?*"

Bonnie Brown looked at Wesley. It was a rare opportunity when she was in such a good negotiating position with her son. She saw the makings of a deal.

"Did you say you will *never* ask me to go see wrestling again?"

"Never. I promise."

"What about all those wrestling magazines?"

"I'll throw them away."

"And the T-shirts?"

"I'll give them to charity."

"Wrestling on TV?"

"I'll never watch it again. I promise."

"I'll have to get that in writing, Wesley."

"No problem."

"You've got a deal."

"Okay, let's go, Mom!"

"Right now?"

"The show starts in half an hour!"

23

The Main Event

WESLEY AND HIS MOTHER DASHED OUT OF the house and raced over to Jimmy's to pick up the tickets. When they knocked on the door, Jimmy was lying on the couch with an ice pack on his knee.

"I've got it all figured out," Jimmy explained. "I bet you Doctor Demented is going to pull off the mask, and there's going to be *another* mask underneath. It's perfect!"

"No way," Wesley insisted. "They'd never let him get away with that."

By the time Wesley and his mother arrived at the Astrodome, there were only a few spots left in the back of the parking lot. Wesley wanted to make a dash for the entrance, but he had to wait for his mother. She grabbed a paperback book from the trunk of the car and slipped it in her purse.

"It will give me something to do when I get bored," she explained.

The preliminary fights were over by the time Wesley and his mother found their seats at ringside.

"You missed some good stuff," said the guy sitting next to them. "They had a steel cage casket match."

"We just came for the main event," Wesley replied.

Suddenly the lights dimmed and four explosions of orange fire shot into the air. Everybody turned to face the main entrance to see what was going to happen. Two rockets were launched. Lasers and colored spotlights spun around the Astrodome. Heavy metal music blasted and smoke machines pumped out thick fog.

Dr. Demented stepped into the main spotlight and the crowd exploded in sound. His muscular body filled the twenty-foot video screens that had been placed around the arena to give the fans a better view.

"Ladies and gentleman," boomed the announcer, "this is the moment you have all been waiting for. It is time for our main event of the evening. From Death Valley, Nevada . . . weighing 250 pounds . . . Doctorrrrrrrrrrrrrrr . . . Demented!"

"Booooooooooooooooooooooo!"

"Yayyyyyyyyyyyyyyyyyyyy," shouted Wesley Brown. His mother opened up her book and began to read it.

Dr. Demented marched slowly up the aisle and stepped between the ropes into the ring. While the boos rained down on him, he scanned the crowd, spotting Wesley with his mother in the front row.

"If Doctor Demented loses this match," the announcer bellowed, "he will have to remove the mask that has hidden his face and his true identity for the past five years."

"Yeaaaaaaaaaaaaaaaaaaahhhhhhhhhh!"

Usually, right after his introduction, Dr. Demented would grab the microphone from the announcer and shout his trademark catchphrase. This time, he didn't do it. The announcer looked at him, puzzled.

"Was there anything you wanted to say, Doctor Demented?"

Dr. Demented shook his head no.

"I . . . RULE . . . THIS . . . PATHETIC . . . WORLD" the crowd chanted without him.

More explosions of orange fire shot out of the main entrance, followed by fireworks, lasers, and smoke.

"And from Tarzana, California," the announcer shouted, "weighing 265 pounds . . . ready, willing, and able to squash bugs wherever he finds them. . . .The Exterrrrrrrrrrrrrrrrminator!"

"Booooooooooooooooooooooo!"

The Exterminator, a black man, was even bigger than Dr. Demented. He was wearing a red satin robe with a picture of a dead cockroach on the back. He flipped off the robe and flexed his shiny muscles for the crowd.

Landon Wheeler looked across the ring as The Exterminator climbed between the ropes. There was something familiar about him. It took a moment or two, but then he realized what it was. The Exterminator was Rick Robinson, the guy from Michigan State who had beaten him out of a spot on the Olympic wrestling team. They hadn't seen each other in years.

The referee signaled both men to join him in the middle of the ring so he could go over the rules. Nobody ever listened to the rules, but this was an opportunity for the wrestlers to stare each other down and create tension for the fans.

"Rick," Mr. Wheeler said, ignoring the ref. "Remember me? Landon Wheeler."

The Exterminator peered at Dr. Demented's mask.

"Sure I remember you," he replied. "The Wheel. We fought for the Olympic spot."

"It's been a long time, Rick."

"Real long."

"Didn't you used to call yourself Terminator?"

"Yeah. I got sued by the studio that made that movie. So I changed it to *E*xterminator. Did you read the script?"

"Yeah."

"When was the last time you jobbed, Wheel?"

"When you beat me at the Olympic trials."

"No kiddin'?" asked The Exterminator. "Lucky me, huh? Listen, I was thinkin' we could have you smack me around for about six minutes, throw me out of the ring, then we get back in here and I'll whip you good. My usual finishing move is an elbow drop into a neckbreaker. You okay with that?"

"No, Rick, I'm not," Landon Wheeler replied.

"Huh?"

"I'm not going to hit you, Rick."

"You're kidding, right?" The Exterminator laughed.

By this time, the referee had finished going over the rules and told the men to go to their corners. In the back of the arena, an AWF official stood around, just to make sure things went according to instructions.

"I'm totally serious," Landon Wheeler said. "I won't hit you."

"But the script says—"

"I don't care what the script says. I'm not playing along anymore."

"They'll stop the fight, Wheel. They'll fire you."

"I don't care."

The referee moved between the two men and shoved them gently in the direction of their corners. The AWF official watched, concern showing on his face.

"So what are you gonna do," The Exterminator asked as he backed toward his corner, "just stand there and let me beat on you?"

"No, I'm going to wrestle."

"Huh?"

"You know, like we did back in college. Folk-style wrestling."

"You're out of your mind, Wheel!"

The clang of the bell ended the discussion. Dr. Demented and The Exterminator came back from their corners and circled around each other in the middle of the ring.

Dr. Demented stopped and balanced his weight in an even stance, the classic amateur wrestling starting position. Feet spread, hands at waist level, weight balanced on a firm base of support.

"Aw, cut that out, Wheel!" said The Exterminator. "You're making a fool of yourself."

Dr. Demented shook his head no.

"You can do whatever you want," The Exterminator declared. "But I've got a job to do."

"Then *do* it."

The Exterminator charged at Dr. Demented, bounced off the ropes and threw a flying dropkick. Ordinarily, the other wrestler lets the boot hit him in the chest and tumbles backward. But Dr. Demented simply stepped out of the way. The Exterminator crashed to the mat on his back.

The fans, assuming that one of the wrestlers had messed up, hooted with laughter.

The Exterminator looked at Dr. Demented as he got up, a puzzled expression on his face. He charged again, this time striking at Dr. Demented with lefts and rights to the head. Ordinarily, a wrestler getting attacked will snap his head back with each blow and fall backward dramatically to heighten the effect. But Dr. Demented easily blocked the punches with his arms and danced away.

A few of the fans in the crowd had already sensed that something was wrong. *He's not fighting back*, Wesley Brown thought to himself.

"Come on, Wheel!" The Exterminator urged. "Hit me or something."

"No."

"You're making me look bad!"

"Then wrestle me," Landon Wheeler dared.

The two men circled around each other some more and Dr. Demented began pommeling—trying to gain upper body position by grabbing at his opponent's hands and arms.

"You never got over the Olympics, did you?" The Exterminator whispered.

"No, I guess I didn't."

"You know, I could beat you again, Wheel."

"Let's see you try."

The Exterminator lowered his hips, trying to pop underneath so he could penetrate Demented's defenses and do a lift. If he could get Demented's feet off the mat, he'd have no base of support.

A murmur had begun to spread through the crowd. By now, the audience would have expected to see one of the wrestlers leap off the ropes or throw the other guy out of the ring and have him crash through a table. So far neither The Exterminator nor Dr. Demented had done anything particularly exciting.

"*Booooooooooooooooooooooo!*" a few people shouted.

"*Borrrrrrrrrrrrrrriinggg!*"

"*Do* something!" a fan screamed.

"This is a ripoff!"

Dr. Demented attempted a double-leg takedown. The Exterminator countered by blocking with one knee, powering his hips forward and arching his back. Dr. Demented cleared him off the mat, straightening The Exterminator up.

The referee looked on nervously. It had been nearly ten years since he had worked an amateur wrestling match. He barely remembered the difference between a snapdown and a look-away.

"What do you guys think you're doing?" the referee complained.

"Wrestling," both men replied.

They continued to struggle for position, going through an intricate series of moves and holds they had practiced so many times back in high school and college. It all came back.

Bonnie Brown glanced up from her book. She was more than a little surprised to see Dr. Demented doing a crossface, controlling The Exterminator's head by reaching across his jaw to his far shoulder. It was a classic wrestling hold she remembered from cheering on her ex-husband so many years ago.

"Why aren't they hitting each other?" she asked Wesley.

"Beats me, Mom."

"He should fake a tie-up, change levels to make a quick penetration underneath, then get him with a double leg attack."

Wesley looked at his mother in shock.

"It's obvious," Bonnie explained. "Just post and drive. If he rolls out, you just counter with a half-nelson."

"Since when do *you* know so much about wrestling?" he asked.

"Your father was a college wrestler," she informed him.

My father was a wrestler. Suddenly, a lot of things made more sense to Wesley Brown. Like, why his mother hated professional wrestling so much. Like why she was down on weight training and building muscles. Like why she was so anti-violence.

My father was a wrestler, and they didn't get along.

"Come on, Demented!" Bonnie Brown shouted. "Go for the lateral drop!"

As the two men grappled for position, a funny thing happened. A buzz moved through the crowd. The boos faded away. Little by little, the fans realized what was going on. These guys weren't faking it. They were wrestling for *real.*

"Get him, Exterminator!" somebody hollered.

"Come on, Doctor Demented!"

People began shouting advice. Scattered cheering began to be heard around the Astrodome.

Dr. Demented grabbed hold of The Exterminator's right hand while moving his right foot toward him. He grabbed Exterminator quickly with his other hand around the back and thrust his hips forward. Arching his back, Demented carried The Exterminator over him and threw him to the mat. The ref held up two fingers to indicate a takedown and two points for Dr. Demented.

"Yeahhhhhhh!"

The AWF official who had been standing in the back of the arena didn't like what he was seeing. The AWF paid Dr. Demented and The Exterminator to brawl, not to have an amateur wrestling match. He raced to the ring, climbed between the ropes, and grabbed The Exterminator.

"That's it!" he shouted. "Stop the fight!"

The Exterminator picked up the AWF guy and sent him flying over the top rope and out of the ring. The crowd roared with approval.

The wrestlers pommeled until Dr. Demented was able to grab The Exterminator's legs and take him down in a double-leg attack. Two more points for Demented. The Exterminator, on the mat now, cut back with his right arm as he increased his back pressure by lifting his hips off the mat. Then he turned on top of Dr. Demented to escape. The move is called a hip switch. The Ref held up two fingers. Two points for The Exterminator.

"Nice reversal," Bonnie Brown commented to Wesley.

"You're better than you were in college," The Exterminator grunted to Dr. Demented.

"So are you."

The Exterminator forced Demented down and applied a half-nelson to him. His left arm was under Dr. Demented's arm and up over his neck. Demented captured the arm in the crook of his elbow to break the pressure. Then he squeezed his elbow tightly into his body and started to do a wing roll.

The Exterminator struggled to hold position, but Dr. Demented had leverage. Exterminator, seeing he couldn't stop the wing roll, tried to use the momentum to roll through it. Dr. Demented wasn't going to fall for that. He stepped over to gain position. The Exterminator was on his back, his shoulders to the mat.

He grunted, trying to roll out, but it was hopeless. It was a solid pin. The referee slapped the mat three times and the crowd just about tore the place down.

The ref held Dr. Demented's hand up in the air. The crowd rose to its feet and gave a standing ovation as Dr. Demented and The Exterminator shook hands.

The announcer climbed into the ring, looking

confused and somewhat upset. Dr. Demented grabbed the microphone out of his hand.

"I want to say something," he hollered over the applause. "*That* was wrestling. *Real* wrestling."

"*Yeaaaaaaaaaaaahhhhhhhhhh!*"

"People, I've been wearing this mask for five years," Dr. Demented continued. "I said I'd take it off if I lost this match. Well, I didn't lose. But I'm going to take it off anyway."

"*Yeaaaaaaaaaaaahhhhhhhhhh!*"

"We can beat the traffic out of the parking lot if we go now," Bonnie Brown suggested to Wesley.

"Mom, you might want to watch this."

Dr. Demented handed the microphone to The Exterminator. Then he reached around the back of his head and began to untie the intricate series of laces and straps that held his mask on. As he worked on the laces, silence fell over the arena.

And then Dr. Demented tore the mask off his face.

Bonnie Brown's shriek could be heard throughout the Astrodome.

"Landon?" she choked weakly.

Involuntarily, Bonnie rose to her feet, then fell back as her knees buckled under her. Wesley caught her before she fell down.

"He's my gym teacher!" somebody shouted.

Landon Wheeler took the microphone and went to the side of the ring where Wesley and his mother were sitting. At the ropes, he sank to his knees.

"I always said I would never get down on my knees before anyone," he said in a hushed voice. "But I'm on my knees now for you, Bonnie."

"Yeahhhhhhhhhh!"

"Get up, Mom!"

Bonnie Brown struggled to her feet. An AWF cameraman rushed over and suddenly Bonnie was twenty feet tall on every video screen around the Astrodome. Guys in the audience began doing wolf whistles.

"Bonnie," Landon Wheeler said softly. "I want you to know two things. First, I love you."

More wolf whistles and hoots from the guys in the crowd.

"The second thing is this. Bonnie, I swear to you, right now, I will never, *ever* hit another human being, for the rest of my life."

The fans erupted into good-natured guffawing at that. The idea of Dr. Demented—the homicidal maniac—turning nonviolent was just the kind of wacky angle those AWF scriptwriters would dream up.

"I *mean* it!" Landon Wheeler thundered.

The crowd shut up.

"I have something else to say. Bonnie, will you marry me?"

The crowd exploded into cheers. Even the AWF official who had been tossed out of the ring was smiling. He hadn't seen this much heat since Dr. Demented ripped that guy's ear off and ate it.

Bonnie Brown turned to look at Wesley. He shrugged his shoulders, as if to say, "It's not up to me."

The Exterminator ripped one of the straps off the Dr. Demented mask and tied it into a simple, but serviceable engagement ring. He handed it to Landon Wheeler, who was still on his knees.

"Say yes! Say yes! Say yes!" the crowd chanted.

Bonnie Brown climbed up into the ring. She wrapped her arms around Landon Wheeler's neck and whispered one word into his ear.

"Yes."

Afterword . . .

IN THE END, THE AWF LOVED WHAT HAD happened. The TV ratings for the Astrodome show had been enormous. Fans deluged AWF offices with phone calls, letters, e-mails, and faxes demanding more of the new unmasked Dr. Demented and "that woman he asked to marry him."

The AWF offered Bonnie Brown and Landon Wheeler a contract to travel around and put on the same performance every week at arenas across the United States.

They turned it down, of course. Instead, they went out and got *real* rings and got married.

Landon Wheeler was accepted to medical school and quit teaching. Between his savings and Bonnie's, they were able to pay the bills. *People* magazine even did an article about him. "From Heel to Healer," it was titled.

Jimmy's knee got better slowly, and Carl Campanella eventually recovered, too. He was still a jerk, but a kinder, gentler jerk. It was obvious that his heart wasn't into harassing people anymore. Carl spent a lot of time looking up in the air, as if something was going to fall on him.

Wesley Brown broke his promise to his mother about giving up everything to do with wrestling. The next year at school, he tried out for the wrestling team and made it.

That same year, Wesley took a biology class. He spent a lot of time learning how muscles worked and looking at animal tissue samples under microscopes. Wesley began thinking he might like to become a doctor someday.

Like his stepdad.

About the Author

Don't tell anyone, but Dan Gutman (270 pounds of rippling muscle capable of tearing a man's head off with one hand) secretly wrestles under the name *The Mortician*. You would never know, as he performs in disguise.

When he is not inflicting punishment and humiliation on the pathetic wimps and crybabies he faces in the ring, Dan writes entertaining middle grade novels such as *The Kid Who Ran for President*, *Honus & Me*, *The Million Dollar Shot*, *The Edison Mystery*, and others.

Dan lives in a steel cage in Haddonfield, New Jersey, with his tag team partner, Nina (known on the wrestling circuit as *The Illustrator*), and their two children, Slam and Enemy.

The only way to see Dan without his mask is at www.dangutman.com.

HEX

IT WAS A BRILLIANT SCIENTIFIC BREAKTHROUGH.
A GENE THAT MUTATES THE MIND,
THAT GIVES A HUMAN BRAIN ACCESS
TO ALL COMPUTER SYSTEMS.

IT IS A DEADLY CURSE. IT CREATES PEOPLE
OF INCALCULABLE POWER, WHO MUST BE
DESTROYED BEFORE THEY CAN GROW UP.

IT IS A THRILLER THAT BLASTS YOU
INTO A MIND-BLOWING FUTURE....

HEX
SHE IS ALL-POWERFUL.
SHE MUST BE DESTROYED!

HEX: SHADOWS
SHE SHOULD BE DEAD.
BUT COMPUTERS ARE HARD TO KILL...
(COMING IN FEBRUARY 2002)

HEX: GHOSTS
THE GOVERNMENT WANTED THEM DEAD.
THE WORLD WAS NOT READY FOR THEM.
BUT NOW THEY ARE GOING
TO MAKE PEOPLE LISTEN.
(COMING IN JUNE 2002)

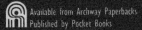
Available from Archway Paperbacks
Published by Pocket Books

3115

Don't Miss a Single Play!

Archway Paperbacks Brings You the Greatest Games, Teams, and Players in Sports!

By

Bill Gutman

☆Football Super Teams

☆Bo Jackson: A Biography

☆Michael Jordan: A Biography (revised)

☆Baseball Super Teams

☆Great Quarterbacks of the NFL

☆Tiger Woods: A Biography

☆ Ken Griffey, Jr.: A Biography

☆ Brett Favre: A Biography

☆Sammy Sosa: A Biography

☆Shaquille O'Neal: A Biography (revised)

An Archway Paperback
Published by Pocket Books

William Corlett's

THE MAGICIAN'S HOUSE QUARTET

Thirteen-year-old William Constant and his two younger sisters, Mary and Alice, have come to ancient, mysterious Golden House in Wales for the holidays. Their lives will never be the same once they enter the Magician's House—and discover their destiny.

THE STEPS UP THE CHIMNEY
What evil lurks in Golden House? The children know....

William knew something was wrong from the moment they arrived at the railroad station on the border of Wales. First came the stranger who said his name was Steven. "Remember me," he said. Then he vanished. By the time they reached Golden House, even Mary and Alice felt something odd. Who—or what—are the strange animals...a fox, a dog, an owl...that seem to be able to read their minds? Why is it that sometimes the children even see out of the eyes of the animals and hear with their ears? And what is that prickling sensation pulling them toward the secret steps up the chimney? Nothing can stop them as they are drawn deep into the old house, into the realm of the Magician.

THE DOOR IN THE TREE
It's even more dangerous when the magic is real....

It's vacation again—time for William, Mary, and Alice to return to Golden House. They've made a solemn vow not to speak of anything that happened on their last visit to Uncle Jack's home. Was the magic real? It seems like a dream to William and Mary. Only Alice knows the secret of magic: believing. It is Alice who discovers the Dark and Dreadful Path, Alice who is irresistibly drawn into the ancient yew tree. And it is Alice who finds the door in the tree—leading to the secret hiding place of the Magician. *It wasn't a dream!*

Soon they've become the Magician's students, led by the kestrel, the badgers, and the dog into the most perilous assignment of all....

And coming in the fall of 2001:
THE TUNNEL BEHIND THE WATERFALL
THE BRIDGE IN THE CLOUDS